MY DOG ATE IT

Weekly Reader Book Club Presents

MY DOG ATE IT

Saragail Katzman Benjamin

Holiday House/New York

This book is a presentation of Newfield Publications, Inc.
Newfield Publications offers book clubs for children from
preschool through high school. For further information
write to: **Newfield Publications, Inc.,**
4343 Equity Drive, Columbus, Ohio 43228.

Published by arrangement with Holiday House.
Newfield Publications is a federally registered trademark
of Newfield Publications, Inc.
Weekly Reader is a federally registered trademark
of Weekly Reader Corporation.

Library of Congress Cataloging-in-Publication Data
Benjamin, Saragail Katzman.
My dog ate it / Saragail Katzman Benjamin.—1st ed.
p. cm.
Summary: Danny's decision to flunk the fifth grade deliberately is
complicated when his teacher anonymously sends him a magical
talking dog to do his homework for him.
ISBN 0-8234-1047-1
[1. Homework—Fiction. 2. Schools—Fiction. 3.Teachers—Fiction.
4. Magic—Fiction.] I. Title.
PZ7.B4349My   1994   93-25218   CIP   AC
[Fic]—dc20

Acknowledgments

I would like to thank my young friends and grown-up colleagues who read this book while it was in progress—Aaron Marx, Jennifer Robeson, Lauren Weintraub, Daniel Laikind, Donna Laikind, Erica Sacken, Lucy Coolidge, Libby Saines, Marni Goltsman, Jane Blumberg, Claudine Cassan-Jellison, Susan Deem, Neil Waldman, Alan Lefkowitz, and Alison Hubbard. I am grateful for their excellent suggestions, and for their enthusiasm and support. I must also thank Rose Turk of the Hillside Diner, who gave me a nice out-of-the-way table and plenty of decaf while I worked on the first draft of this book.

I extend a very special thanks to Carole Kelley and her 1992–93 fifth grade class at Davis School, New Rochelle, New York.

I would like to thank Dodie Hussey, who so generously allowed me the use of her printer.

I thank my friend and agent, Marilyn Epstein Weintraub, for embarking on this wonderful adventure with me.

I thank Ashley Mason at Holiday House, who rescued my manuscript from a bottomless pile of submissions, and my editor, Margery Cuyler, for her expert help in shaping the book, and for believing in me.

I thank my family—my parents, my in-laws, and my kids, Joshua and Aaron—for loving me and helping me through the process. And I especially thank my husband, Scott, for his insight and patience; who read and responded with such great care to so many revisions of this book it would have made anybody else cuckoo.

Contents

MY DOG ATE IT

CHAPTER

1

WARP, WARP, WARP, WARP

"*SEVEN BELLS! SEVEN BELLS!*" Dad boomed and flashed Danny's bedroom lights on and off, on and off, and on.

"*Eee-YAHHHH!*" Danny screamed as if he'd been jolted with enough electricity to light deep space. He fumbled for the light switch, flicked it off, and slithered back under his covers.

Dad was not a person who was easily discouraged. He reached for the switch and flashed the lights some more, bellowing cheerfully, "*YOU HEARD THE ALARM, DANNY! MONDAY MORNING! SEVEN BELLS! RISE AND SHINE!*"

Danny peeked out from under his covers and glowered at his father.

"Good morning, Danny-Banany!" Dad said.

"I *hate* that!" Danny grumbled. "No fifth grader is called Danny-Banany!"

"Yeah, but it wakes you up, doesn't it?" Dad said. Then he was on his way, eager to torment other unsuspecting family members.

Danny plopped his pillow over his head.

"Seven bells, Evie! Seven bells, Mom!" Dad called. Even with the pillow on his head, Danny could hear his father.

Why does he *do* that? Danny asked himself. *"Seven bells! Seven bells!"* Does he think he's a sea captain? He's not a sea captain. He's a dentist.

Suddenly, Danny's eyes were flooded with light.

"Danny," Mom said, standing over him, holding his pillow. "You're still in bed."

"Yes, Mom," Danny answered. "I *am* in bed."

Mom was very observant. She had to be. Especially about beds. She reported on home furnishings for the newspaper.

Danny reached for his pillow, but Mom pulled it just beyond his grasp.

"Please get up, get washed, and get dressed, Danny," Mom said. "You'll be late for school."

"Mommy! Mommy! Mommy!" Danny's four-year-old sister, Evie, yowled down the hall. She sounded like a wounded goat.

"Yes, Evie, what is it?" Mom called. She left, taking Danny's pillow with her.

"SEVEN BELLS AND TWO MINUTES!" Dad yelled. *"RISE AND SHINE!"*

Time warps, Danny thought. That's the only

explanation. It's like I'm trapped in a science fiction movie about time warps, and there's no escape. One minute I'm sound asleep, the next minute—*WARP!*—I'm being tortured by a dentist who thinks he's a sea captain who likes to blind me with flashing lights. One minute it's the weekend, then—*WARP!*—Mom grabs my pillow off my head and it's Monday-morning-get-dressed-eat-breakfast-go-to-school. Then *WARP*—science, *WARP*—math, *WARP*—colonial America, *WARP*—nouns, *WARP*—verbs, *WARP*—stand up, *WARP*—sit down, sit up, sit still, talk, don't talk, breathe in, breathe out, get in line, go here, go there, go *WARP, WARP, WARP, WARP!* All day long, then *WARP*—home to homework.

And it's important. It's all important. Usually, it's interesting. Sometimes, it's fun. And sometimes, *some*times, it's *too much*. Sometimes, I'd like a three-month Christmas vacation, or a five-day weekend, or maybe just a four-hour gym class. I could perfect my jump shot. But do I have anything to say about it? No. Does anyone ever ask me what *I* think of the schedule? No. Do I have any control over anything at all? Absolutely n—

"PUTTING-ON-SNEAKER BELLS!" Dad yelled up the stairs.

Danny got up, got dressed, and put on his snea—

"Come on now, Danny!" Mom yelled.

WARP, WARP, WARP, WARP. No control over anything at all.

Danny tied his shoes and went downstairs to the usual breakfast scene. Everything was the same as always, with the usual cereal, juice, toast, yogurt, milk, coffee for the grown-ups, and the same slurping and crunching and munching Danny came down to every morning. But one thing was different. Next to Danny's cornflakes there was a form. The words *middle school registration* were printed across the top, and it was all filled out.

"Danny, please take that form to school," Mom said. "It's due back today."

"No," said Danny, scrutinizing the form, "it says here it's not due back till February fifteenth."

Dad checked the date on his digital watch. "Today!" he said. "February fifteenth!"

"Judy would like more milk, please," Evie said.

"Here you go, Judy," said Mom, pouring milk into a cup Evie was holding in front of her favorite doll, Judy. "Please share some with Evie, OK, Judy?"

Judy was made out of orange plastic, and she had ratty, fluorescent, glow-in-the-dark hair that changed colors every fifteen minutes. Danny always had a difficult time not throwing up watching his sister pretend to feed the disgusting toy, but today, it was almost more than he could handle. He took a sip of orange juice and stared at his cornflakes.

"Finish up, Danny," Mom said. "You know you can't go to middle school unless you finish fifth grade first. And at the rate you're going, it'll be June before you finish your orange juice!" She laughed and kissed Danny lightly on the forehead.

"Mom," Danny whined, brushing her away. "I've been asking you to knock that off since third grade!"

"Sorry," said Mom, wiping the kiss off Danny's forehead with a dish towel. "I forgot." She pointed to the form. "This is exciting," she said.

"Middle school," Dad said with a smile. "Terrific."

Terrific, Danny thought, mooshing his cornflakes with his spoon. *WARP, WARP, WARP*—middle school. Everyone said it was the real thing. *Real life.* The middle school kids always carried around thick, loose-leaf notebooks. The notebooks looked cool, they made the kids look smart, with all the different sections, and stuff scribbled all over the covers. But they also looked heavy. Very thick. Lots to do. *"You'll never make it,"* Danny's eighth-grade cousin, Reese, had told him. *"You'll die trying,"* Reese had said. Of course Reese was a jerk, but still, he might have a point. Already, it seemed like there was more and more to do in fifth grade, and less and less time to do it in. Could middle school be much wor—

"Hurry up, Danny!" Mom yelled, looking out the window. "Your bus is here!" Danny gulped the rest of his juice while Mom handed him his jacket and his book bag. Dad shoved a toothbrush in with Danny's books.

"Brush at school," Dad said.

"Right," Danny answered and scrambled for the door.

"Wait!" Mom called. "You forgot your registration form!"

She stuffed that in his book bag, and Danny raced for his bus. He was very quiet on the ride to school.

"What's with you this morning?" his best friend Eric Bedemeyer asked him.

"Just thinking," Danny said.

What was it Mom had said at breakfast? Danny tried to remember. It was just before she kissed him. (Yuck.) Something about cornflakes. No. Something about milk—no—orange juice. That was it. Orange juice. She'd said that he had to finish his orange juice so he could finish fifth grade. And . . . and . . . had she also said that he had to finish fifth grade before he could go to middle school? Had she actually said that?

Maybe he shouldn't have finished his juice. Maybe if he'd sat at the breakfast table sipping and sipping, magically, the juice would have taken him months, even years to finish, and he would have been able to *WARP* ahead to middle school when he was good and ready. No such luck. Still, it was an interesting idea. Worth thinking about.

Once Danny got to school, he knew exactly what to do. He walked through the school doors and found a trash can. He opened his book bag, took out the middle school registration form, crumpled it up, and threw it in the trash. Next he lifted all his homework assignments out of his homework folder and threw them in the trash, too.

Danny took a deep breath and walked to his classroom.

CHAPTER

2

My Dog Ate It

Several weeks later, on a dreary March morning, Danny's ordinary, teacherly looking teacher, Ms. McCardle, was playing fetch with a not-so-ordinary-looking dog in the park.

He was one of those combination dogs. He had the compact, sturdy body of a terrier combined with the head of a beagle; complete with a beagle's big sad eyes, and floppy beagle's ears that flew out and back like jet wings when he ran. His coat was shaggy and wiry; black and tan all over, except for a broad, bushy, black V that stretched across his forehead. It made him look like he had one long black eyebrow that did double duty for both eyes, so that unless you really knew him, he looked like he should be smoking a smelly cigar

8

and saying things like, Life's tough, kid. Can't take de heat, get outta de kitchen!

Today Ms. McCardle, who was usually a pretty good fetch-partner, seemed to be off her throw. That is, when she bothered to throw at all. Mostly, she muttered quietly to herself.

"He's driving me *berserk!*" she muttered now, twisting the fetch-stick around and around in her hands. The dog eyed it wistfully, but Ms. McCardle didn't see him. "The boy makes no sense whatsoever! He just stops? A perfectly good student suddenly does no homework whatsoever? Why?"

"Awrrrrr?" asked her dog. His V-shaped eyebrow turned itself upside-down, making a little thatched roof for his face, and his sad beagle's eyes drooped even lower than usual. He nuzzled Ms. McCardle's leg. Finally, she noticed him.

"I'm awfully sorry, I didn't mean to make you wait so long," she said. "Here you go! One last throw before school!"

She threw the stick, but her aim was wild, and the stick got caught in the upper branches of a tall tree.

"Woof woof ARF!" barked the dog.

"Yes, it *was* a particularly nice stick," said Ms. McCardle. She was nearsighted, and peered through glasses with oversized tortoiseshell frames up into the tree.

"Woof woof bark, woof!" the dog sulked.

"If it's that upsetting to you, why don't you go get it?"

The dog took a deep breath, then without even taking a running start, he leaped about thirty feet into the air. He hovered near the upper branches of the tree while he grabbed the stick in his mouth, then he kind of sat down in midair and began a slow descent.

Ms. McCardle didn't pay any attention to the dog. She was busy muttering again. "He just stops . . . does no homework at all . . . and the excuses he makes—outrageous. Is it time for the *Plan?*"

"WOOF!" barked the dog, dropping the stick proudly at Ms. McCardle's feet.

"Oh!" Ms. McCardle exclaimed, startled. Then she looked at the dog intently. "We may need to implement the *Plan* very soon," she said. "Possibly tonight."

"Arf!" barked the dog.

"I'll talk to the boy one more time in school today, and then we'll see. You know I don't like to use a drastic measure like the *Plan* unless absolutely necessary."

"Arf," said the dog, nodding, and the two friends left the park.

*   *   *

March is too early for flies, Danny thought later that same afternoon at school, yet he had just spotted one.

"Bzz. Bzzzbzzz."

It got lost in Francy Kloss's perm.

"Bzzzzzbzzzbzbzzzzzzzbzzzbzbzbzbzzzzzzzzbzzzzzzzzzzzzzzz!!!!"

It escaped.

It flew over to Eric Bedemeyer's desk—wandered across Missouri in Eric's social studies book—*bzzzzed* over to the American flag in front of the classroom—circled it three times—crash-landed on the bulletin board (on a weird musical note/bluebird kind of animal)—and cleaned its antennae. Very, very carefully. Next stop, the blank sign-up sheet for the Think-Off Contest . . . what was that?

"Danny!"

Someone was calling his name.

"Well, Danny?" Ms. McCardle said. She looked at him as if she expected him to answer a question.

WARP, WARP. Answer a question. What question?

"Ninety-six," Danny answered.

A few kids laughed softly.

"Excuse me, Danny?" Ms. McCardle asked.

"The answer to the problem is ninety-six. Isn't that right?" Danny asked.

More kids laughed, but not Danny's best friend, Eric Bedemeyer. Eric was a straight-*A* student. He tried to whisper the correct answer to Danny, but Ms. McCardle stopped him.

"Eric Bedemeyer, if you bail your friend out one more time, he's never going to learn to think for himself."

Eric was silent.

"Danny, the starting point of the Oregon Trail is not ninety-six," Ms. McCardle continued. "We finished math an hour ago."

Danny remembered the fly walking across Missouri in Eric's social studies book and felt silly for not doing a slicker job of faking it.

"I think the answer you're looking for is Trail Town," Danny said. "Yes. Trail Town is definitely the starting point of the Oregon Trail."

The whole class broke up, everyone except Eric and Ms. McCardle. They just stared at Danny in disbelief.

"Danny, may I please see your social studies homework for today?" said Ms. McCardle.

"Right now?" Danny asked.

"Right now."

"I'd like to show it to you. In fact, I worked real hard on it, and I was going to ask my mom to write me a note, because . . ." Danny paused, stalling. The whole class was silent, dying to know what excuse he was going to use this time.

"My dog ate it."

The class went crazy.

"You used that one *last* week!" Tommy Lewis called out. "And we *all* know you don't . . ."

Here the whole class joined in. *"HAVE* a dog!"

Ms. McCardle silenced them all with a look they called her "kill-look." Her glasses, with their oversized frames, just seemed to intensify the effect. The kids shut up. Only Tommy Lewis kept giggling for awhile and earned himself what the kids called a "double whammy," that is, a kill-look combined with Ms. McCardle's highly arched left eyebrow. The eyebrow sort of lifted up and peeked over her glasses.

"Danny, please come to my desk," Ms. McCardle said in a quiet, controlled voice. "The rest of the class will please open their English books to Chapter 11 and start their homework."

WARP, WARP—come to my desk. WARP, WARP— teacher write a note home. What a nice little song, Danny thought, walking up to Ms. McCardle's desk, and he sang it to himself again. *WARP, WARP— come to my desk. WARP, WARP—teacher write a note home. But she can't catch me, 'cuz I'm WARP-FREE!!!* Yep, there she goes, she's reaching for the drawer, that was the one, second on the left, now here it comes, here it comes, here's the school stationery, there's the pen—*scribble, scribble, scratch, scratch*—in that funny, old-fashioned kind of handwriting she had.

"I'd like you to take this note to your parents,"

Ms. McCardle said as she folded the note and put it in an envelope.

"Sure, Ms. McCardle," Danny said pleasantly. He stuffed the note in his pocket and started strolling away.

"Danny!" she called, and he strolled back.

"Doesn't it bother you to do so poorly in school?" Ms. McCardle asked.

No answer.

"Your work used to be so much better," Ms. McCardle continued. "In fact, you actually used to *do* your work."

Ms. McCardle paused. Danny nodded politely.

"I've written notes to your parents before, and when I do, things improve for a few days, but that's all," said Ms. McCardle. "The school psychologist has interviewed you and she says you're very happy. Are you happy, Danny?"

Danny nodded and smiled.

"HOW CAN YOU POSSIBLY BE HAPPY WHEN YOU'RE FLUNKING!?!" Ms. McCardle snapped, but she quickly regained her composure. "Forgive me for raising my voice," she said quietly, "but this is very frustrating for me. I'm your friend. I want to help you, but I can't unless you let me. Is there anything you want to tell me?"

Danny was silent.

"You see, Danny, it's already getting on to the

end of March, and if I don't see some improvement soon, I won't be able to pass you. I know you don't want to stay in fifth grade next year while all your friends move on to sixth grade and middle school."

"Yeah, middle school," Danny said. "You know, fifth grade isn't so bad, and who knows, there may be some nice kids in here next year. I bet I'll make some good new friends. Then I'll have friends in this class *and* in middle school."

Ms. McCardle stared at him. "You *can't* be serious, Danny."

"Oh yeah," Danny replied. "I'll get to middle school sooner or later. No need to rush. Life goes fast enough."

"What do you mean, *fast?*" asked Ms. McCardle, looking at him curiously.

"Fast," Danny answered. "You know, the opposite of, umm . . . *slow.*"

Ms. McCardle considered this information for a moment in silence. "Mm," she finally said, gazing out over her classroom. Not one of her students was reading Chapter 11 as requested. They were all staring at her and at Danny, watching them like a movie. A quick kill-look, and twenty-one heads were buried in English books. "Mmmmmmm," Ms. McCardle said, turning back to Danny. "Well. Please give the note to your parents."

Just then the bell rang, ending classes for the

day. The kids exploded out of their chairs, grabbed their books, and hurtled toward the door. They paused just long enough to tease Danny. The kids barked, they howled, they panted. Tommy Lewis pretended to be a dog vomiting up homework and grossed out all the girls.

"Ooooooooh!" they squealed.

Danny laughed and pretended to vomit homework too.

"Ooooooooh! OOOOOOOOOOOH!" went the girls.

"Everyone, please pick up a health form on your way out!" Ms. McCardle called over the hubbub. "The middle school office needs them in two weeks! And don't forget to sign up for the Great Think-Off Contest!" She tapped the sign-up sheet, but nobody paid any attention. The bell had rung, and the kids were free.

Eric Bedemeyer worked his way over to Danny.

"Let's go home and shoot some baskets," Danny suggested, slapping Eric on the back.

"What about the note?" asked Eric.

"What note?" said Danny.

"The note Ms. McCardle just gave you to give your parents!"

"Oh yeah. I forgot."

"Are you kidding? Come on, Danny, she could really flunk you!"

Danny laughed. "Big deal, I'll flunk!" he said, but Eric looked so worried that Danny finally went to his desk and got some books to take home. "Feel better?" he asked Eric.

"I'll help you," offered Eric.

"I'll be fine," Danny said, then he jumped up, caught an invisible basketball, and dribbled it out of the room.

"You forgot your health form!" Eric called after him.

"You take mine!" Danny called back.

"What could I possibly want with two health forms?" Eric asked, but Danny couldn't hear him. Danny was already halfway down the hall.

Eric shook his head and trudged after him, certain that his friend was doomed to spend the rest of his natural life in Ms. McCardle's fifth grade.

The Plan for the Improving of Homework

Ms. McCardle may have looked ordinary enough, but she definitely had an unusual dog. And she had an extremely unusual house.

First of all, there was the furniture. All of it had legs and hairy little feet. *Real* legs and *real* feet. When Ms. McCardle went to sit down, the chair or the couch she was heading for would walk forward a couple of inches and lift up a bit to meet her. The dining table, in the dining alcove at one side of the room, was even more helpful, since it had hands, too. she had dinner at the table, when the meal the whole table would walk into the itself, and do the dishes. Very eous furniture, Ms. McCardle had. the books. They were every-oo many to be contained on shelves, so Ms. McCardle had neatly stacked the overflow on the furniture, under the furniture, and around the furniture in colorful book mountains and islands. There were books in every language currently in use, and some in languages that haven't been heard for hundreds of years, not anywhere close by, anyway.

The best part was that if Ms. McCardle opened a book when the weather was chilly, a nice hot cup of cocoa and a plate of oatmeal cookies would instantly materialize, and the book would read itself to her in a comforting, grandmotherly voice. In summertime, she got fresh lemonade and ice cream.

The walls of the room were covered with beautiful paintings, most of them portraits of Ms. McCardle. *Woman Standing Before the Blackboard,* by Picasso; *Teacher and a Bowl of Fruit in the Playground,* by Renoir; and so on. Then there was a picture of Washington crossing the Delaware with an inscription on the bottom that read, The unit on compasses was very helpful. Respectfully yours—Georgie.

On the piano there was some music titled, The Ms. McCardle Sonata, by L. V. Beethoven. On the coffee table there was a pile of old homework assignments. The top one had a speech that began, "To be, or to be . . ." It was marked in red, " 'To be or *not* to be,' might work better. Try it—Ms. McC."

But perhaps the most unusual thing in the room was sitting near the edge of Ms. McCardle's desk.

There, right next to the paper clips, was an apple. It was much larger than any apple any student could have given her, even at the height of an excellent apple season, and it glowed with a red more lustrous than any kid could have gotten by polishing it with his or her jacket on the bus. This was because it was not a real apple. It was a giant jewel, made of gold, covered with layers and layers of translucent red enamel. On one side, golden letters in an ancient, flowing script spelled the word, *Teacher,* and on the other side, smaller letters in the same script formed this message:

I henceforth bequeath thee the apple, the Manual, and the dog.
May they be tools to fulfilling thine own potential,
And may fortune smile on your teaching endeavors.

> Love, Mother
> September 9, 1571

The apple rested on top of a well-worn booklet with the words, *Plan for the Improving of Homework,* written across the cover in the same ancient script. Next to it was a dog's leash and collar. No tags.

It was a far from ordinary living room, full of far from ordinary things, and the afternoon that Danny had insisted the starting point of the Oregon Trail was Trail Town, Ms. McCardle was far from ordinarily upset. She arrived home from school and ignored her wonderful books, and her beautiful paintings, and the special music written just for her.

"Homework! Homework!" she called. She looked around. "Homework! Where are you?" No one answered. She walked over to her desk and tossed down her things. She took her beautiful, red-enameled apple and raised it high with her left hand. Then, with the pointer finger of her right hand, she drew circles in the air around it three times. While she drew, she chanted slowly,

> "Homework, oh Homework,
> Whither dost thou roam?
> Homework, sweet canine,
> Prithee, hie thee home!"

Nothing happened. She tried again, only she was getting a little impatient. The circles ended up looking more like hexagons or lopsided rectangles, and the slow chant rattled along like a rap song.

Once again, nothing happened.

"After four or five hundred years these things just aren't worth a hoot," she muttered, and set the apple down.

She tromped into the kitchen, grabbed a dog biscuit out of a box, and held it up in the air. Immediately, Homework bounded into the room and jumped on her, barking and wagging his tail.

"Always works," Ms. McCardle said, chuckling. She gave the dog his treat.

"Woof wow bow?" Homework asked, spraying a few crumbs on the floor.

"We start the *Plan* today," Ms. McCardle said quietly, then she said nothing more. Absentmindedly, she took her glasses off to polish them, and when she was done, she put them on Homework as if she thought he needed glasses too.

"Herr, herr, herr," laughed Homework. He loved it when Ms. McCardle did that.

"Oh, sorry," said Ms. McCardle, taking her glasses back. Then she put them in the microwave.

"Woof!" barked Homework, pointing to the oven.

"Oh, thank you," said Ms. McCardle, retrieving her glasses. "Remember what happened the last time!"

"RRR rrrRRR rrr!" went Homework as he shook violently and jumped all over the place, pretending to be a pair of glasses exploding in a microwave.

"Ha ha ha!" laughed Ms. McCardle.

"Herr herr herr!" laughed Homework. Then more thoughtfully, he asked, "Woof werr?" He knew Ms. McCardle only made these little mistakes with her glasses when she was particularly worried about something.

"I *am* a little worried, actually, Homework," Ms. McCardle said. "I didn't want to bring it up until I was sure I had an assignment for you. I don't quite know how to put this, Homework. I don't want to hurt your feelings, but I'm worried about you."

"Arf arf?" the dog asked, quite surprised.

"I want you to be very . . . well, let's see, umm . . . *careful* on this assignment," Ms. McCardle said.

"Arr werr rarr rarr ROOF!" responded Homework indignantly.

"I know you're always careful, and I know you try very, very hard, but really, Homework, the last couple of assignments have gotten, umm, a little *confused,* that's the word, a little *confused,*" said Ms. McCardle.

"ARR ARF!!!" Homework was outraged.

"Now, now, no reason to get upset," Ms. McCardle said.

"Arr arf," he repeated.

"Now, Homework, please listen carefully. Danny, the boy you will be helping, believes that if he flunks fifth grade he won't have to grow up. This has been a very common problem through the ages and is best handled adhering strictly to our standard *Plan for the Improving of Homework.* Now, due to your *own* problem, this problem you're having with uh, er . . . *confusion,* I think we should review the *Plan.*"

"Grr," Homework growled softly. He made a point of looking away from Ms. McCardle.

Ms. McCardle made a point of ignoring him, and went on. "Stick to the *Plan*. First of all, encourage good feelings in Danny by doing his homework for him. Improved grades build self-esteem. Improved self-esteem will make Danny want to grow up. At the same time, encourage Danny to work on his own. This way, his good feelings will grow out of his own efforts and he will soon be totally independent, confident that he can handle the normal stresses of life."

"Roof roo—" Homework started to say, but Ms. McCardle cut him off.

"Oh!" she exclaimed. "I almost forgot. Remember, only get Danny's grades back up to their previous level, the level he usually attained before needing our help—mostly *B*'s, a few *A*'s once in a while. Anything higher, he must achieve on his own."

"*Woof bark bark bark bark arf arf roof,*" Homework barked in a huff.

"Well, I know that's what you *think* you do," Ms. McCardle said sweetly. In fact, her voice had become so disgustingly sweet, just listening to it was starting to give Homework a stomachache. "But I think perhaps," Ms. McCardle went sweetly on, "just perhaps, you feel too sorry for the children you help, and you *confuse* doing the child's work *for* him or her with getting the child to work on *his or her own.* Is that possible, Homework?"

Homework looked at Ms. McCardle for a moment, then said quietly, "Arf arf woof woof, arf arf wow wow bow bow, bark arf erf."

"What?" asked Ms. McCardle.

"Arf arf woof woof, arf arf wow wow bow bow, bark arf erf," the dog repeated, a little louder this time.

"Outdated?" said Ms. McCardle. She laughed. "What a silly idea. The *Plan for the Improving of Homework* has worked for hundreds of years, and it will work now."

"Erf er—" Homework started to say, but Ms. McCardle interrupted him.

"Now, now," she said. "You just needed a little review, that's all." Ms. McCardle reached down and scratched Homework's ears.

Homework looked up at her and nodded vaguely. He loved having his ears scratched. It was difficult for him to think clearly when he was having his ears scratched.

"Are you upset because I said I was worried about your performance on the *Plan*?" Ms. McCardle asked.

"Ararf . . ." Homework started to say, but in the middle of his sentence, Ms. McCardle happened to find an especially hard-to-reach spot on his head. The dog rolled his eyes in appreciation.

"Just as I thought," said Ms. McCardle. "You know, Homework, I think you're basically an excellent homework dog, and to prove my faith in you, I'll let you wait the usual three weeks to check in with me. Is that better now?" She gave Homework a big smile.

The dog looked up at her with a contented, dazed expression.

"And now, I guess you might as well be going!" Ms. McCardle said. "Good-bye! And good luck!"

She bent down and gave Homework a big hug, then together, they walked into the living room. Homework sat down in the middle of the living room rug, while Ms. McCardle went over to her desk. She picked up her beautiful, red-enameled apple in her left hand. With the pointer finger of her right hand, she drew three circles in the air around the apple. While she drew, she chanted softly:

"Help the boy, gain his trust,
'Ere his brain can gather dust!
Canine friend, it's up to you!
Now go, go, go! And do, do, do!"

With one last whimper and a wag of his tail, Homework was gone.

4

Two Dragons and a Grasshopper

*D*essert that night was the whole family's favorite—chocolate double fudge layer cake. Danny, his mom, his dad, and his little sister Evie had just taken their first double fudge bites when the phone rang. Mom got it while everybody else kept eating. Chocolate cake in this house did not wait for anything or anybody. At least not yet.

Mom came back. Upset. They all knew she was upset even before she said anything because her lips were pursed and she was making little huffing sounds, like a dragon warming up for fire-snorting. Whenever she was upset, she pursed and huffed, and that night she did so with great determination.

"Danny, do you have something to show your father and me?" Mom asked. Somehow, her lips managed to stay pursed even while she talked. Then, one more huff.

"Like what, Mom?" Danny asked.

"Like the note Ms. McCardle gave you today in school!" The Mom-dragon was completely warmed up.

WARP, WARP, Danny thought, Mom is mad. He tried singing silently to himself the little song he'd made up in school that day, *WARP, WARP, You can't catch me, 'cuz WARP, WARP, I'm WARP-FREE!* but he didn't even get halfway through. It was a hard song to sing when your mother was a dragon.

Meanwhile, the Dad-dragon came to life. Instead of the short huffs Mom made, Dad did more of a long slow hiss when he was upset with his kids, sort of like a leaky radiator. Dad hissed once, and pushed away his chocolate cake to make more room for his anger.

"Another note?" Dad said, very low and quiet. "I thought this situation had improved."

Danny clutched his fork desperately for a second, as if by holding on to a piece of silverware he could make this current *WARP* disappear. It didn't work. Silverware cannot stop a *WARP*. Danny took one last bite of cake, put his fork on his plate, and pushed it away, like a condemned criminal unable to finish his last meal. Even Evie stopped eating and feeding her Judy doll so she could watch the most messed-up big brother in the whole world.

"I'm sorry Mom and Dad, I just completely forgot about that note. Here it is." Danny reached into his right pocket and dug around. Nothing. Then his left pocket. More nothing. He couldn't find the note. "Maybe it fell out. Maybe I took it out when I was playing basketball."

"When you were doing *WHAT!?!*" This was from the Mom and Dad dragons together. Lots of smoke. Danny thought he saw flames lick the ceiling.

The Dad-dragon went on alone. "You've been told that you are not allowed to play basketball until you are done with your homework, so I'm assuming that since you were playing basketball, tonight's homework is already done."

Danny moved his head slowly from left to right, and right to left to signal no. "I'll bring another note home tomorrow. Sorry 'bout that," he said, as he pushed his chair out and started to leave the table.

"No way!" said Mom. "We're going to sit here and talk this thing out once and for all!"

Danny sat down.

Mom and Dad studied him. The grasshopper must have felt like this, Danny thought, remembering the grasshopper his class had studied and studied until they dissected it. But then grasshoppers were probably too little for dragons to dissect. Dragons would be more likely to squoosh him, but somehow he thought squooshing might be better than the talking-to-*WARP* he knew he was in for.

"You used to be a good student," Mom said.

"Mostly *B*'s, and a few *A*'s, once in awhile," Danny volunteered.

Mom didn't notice. "Mostly *B*'s, a few *A*'s, once in awhile," she said. "A good student. But now . . ." Mom sighed.

Danny wished he could hop away.

"I think it was February, wasn't it, yes, last month, when you began this downward trend," a disappointed Dad-dragon said.

Hop, hop, hop away.

"Has something happened?" Dad asked. "Is something bothering you? Mom and I want to help you, but we can't help if you don't talk to us."

What's bothering me right now is that I'm sitting here stuck in a being-dissected-*WARP* when I'd rather be finishing my cake, Danny wanted to say. But he didn't.

What he said was, "I don't know, I just don't *feel* like doing any more homework. *Ever*."

The dragons watched the grasshopper in silence.

"It's too fast," Danny finally blurted out.

"What's too fast, son?" the Dad-dragon asked. "Are they pushing you too fast at school?"

"No, no, no, that's not it," said Danny. Ms. Mc-Cardle hadn't understood either, Danny thought. Why? It didn't seem that complicated.

The dragons watched their grasshopper and waited for more, but more did not come.

"Then what?" the Mom-dragon asked.

"Well, I don't know, life, I suppose," Danny said.

"What about *life?*" Dad asked.

"*Life*, you know *life* . . . is fast. I mean, now I'm in fifth grade, and pretty soon I'll be in sixth."

Mom interrupted, "Middle school—isn't that exciting?"

"Very exciting," said Danny, not looking excited at all. "Anyway, then I'll go on to seventh grade, then eighth, ninth—high school, college, you know, all grown-up. I think I like fifth grade a lot. Fifth grade is good."

"But you can't stay in fifth grade forever, Danny!" Dad wasn't quite yelling, but he was getting close.

"Naw, naw, naw, not forever," Danny responded. "Maybe a couple of years, then sixth grade for two or three, seventh could probably stand a couple of runs through—things probably get pretty complicated by seventh grade. Then I guess I'll be ready for eighth, and then . . ."

"Daniel, at that rate you will be forty years old before you finish high school!" Dad exclaimed.

"Exactly!" Danny said smiling, and slapped the table in satisfaction. Dad finally understood. Or did he? He was glaring at his socks.

Mom laughed. "Danny, everyone has to grow up, honey, and even if you stayed in fifth grade forever, you'd still be all grown-up eventually." She stopped suddenly, as if something had just struck her. She put an arm around Danny's shoulders. "Are you afraid of going to middle school, honey?" she asked.

"Of course not," Danny said. "Give me a break."

Mom studied him. "That's good, that's very good," she said.

Danny said nothing.

Mom rubbed his back. "You know, sweetie, you're right," she said. "Life *does* go fast, and it's good that you know that at your young age. But since you *do* know that, you might as well try to enjoy your life, instead of trying to stop it."

"Yes," added Dad, "there's nothing you can do to keep from growing up." He patted Danny on the back too.

"And remember," Mom said. "Daddy and I are here to help you all along the way." She hugged Danny, then she took a deep breath. "Now Danny, Ms. McCardle told me what was in the note." Mom's voice was very matter-of-fact and businesslike. Danny knew this was a danger signal. *WARP*,

WARP. Mom was using her punishment voice. She always gave punishments as if she were doing the banking or ordering groceries. *"We'll take that in tens and twenties with a pound of chopped meat and no television for a week, please."*

Mom went on, "Ms. McCardle told me what tonight's assignments are. In fact, she gave me all the homework assignments for the rest of the week." Mom held up a piece of paper with Danny's death sentence scribbled on it in chapters and page numbers.

Dad spoke next. "I think we should tack this [Dad pointed to the paper Mom held] on the bulletin board in the kitchen. If you finish your homework before Mom or I get home from work, show your completed assignments to Grandma, and she'll cross them off the paper."

"But Grandma is *Evie's* babysitter!" Danny couldn't stand it. He loved Grandma, but when she stayed with Danny and Evie after school until Mom or Dad came home from work, she was a *baby*sitter. "I'm too *old* to have a *baby*sitter! You *know* that!" Danny wailed.

Mom and Dad watched Danny patiently while he fell apart, then Dad continued on as before. "The point is, you will have to show your completed homework to Grandma, Mom, or me—whoever's around, before there's any basketball, or TV."

Mom's turn. "Ms. McCardle will call us every Sunday night with the next week's assignments."

Danny felt as if he had been dissected *and* squooshed. "How long will this go on?" he muttered.

"As long as necessary," the dragon-parent-punishment-team chimed together.

"As long as necessary." "It's good for your character." And *"Eat your carrots."* These and other key phrases must have been included in a booklet of dragon phrases given to all new dragon-parents when they left the hospital with their baby grasshoppers, Danny thought. *For the Better-ification of Your Precious Grasshoppers,* the book must have been called, and his parents must have memorized it page by page, because they recited it together at every opportunity.

"As long as necessary," they said again, and Danny looked ahead to years of bleakness.

Dad's turn again. "And you're grounded."

"With phone or without?" Danny asked.

"Without," Mom and Dad said together.

"Right," said Danny. "I thought so."

Danny couldn't move. He wanted to move, but he couldn't. Oh yes, I've been dissected, he reminded himself. Even the chocolate cake still waiting on his plate couldn't motivate him. Evie, on the other hand, ignored by everybody, was starting to feed herself and Judy their third piece.

"Get going, honey, before it gets too late," Mom said.

Danny wondered how she could sound so nice when she'd just dissected him. In a daze, he pushed his chair away from the table and stood up. As he walked across the living room and climbed the stairs to his own room, he knew the grown-ups had won. Again. Just like they always did. After all, it was their world, their rules, their *WARPS*. If he didn't do his homework and *WARP* ahead, like he was supposed to do, he would have to stay in grounded-*WARP* forever. What a choice.

He had just arrived at the door to his room, just reached for the doorknob, when he heard something.

"Err," the something went, kind of soft and whiney. And then again, only longer, "Errrrrr."

The sounds seemed to be coming from inside Danny's room.

5

Ooey Kaflooey
Kachoo, Kachoo

"*O*ooey kaflooey kachoo, kachoo. Ooey kaflooey kachoo," Danny whispered to his bedroom door, without really even thinking about what he was saying.

When he was a kid, that was what he had always whispered to the monsters he was sure were hiding under his bed at night, and it had always worked. The monsters had never jumped out at him; never gobbled him down when he got up at night to use the bathroom or get a drink of water. So, when Danny heard strange noises coming from his room, the years of monster-control paid off, and he instinctively knew just what to do.

"Ooey kaflooey kachoo," he whispered once more, then opened the door.

What could have made those noises? A baby? A

dog? Martians? Creatures that would render him powerless to slam dunk, ever, even when he grew the foot the pediatrician had practically guaranteed he would by the time he was eighteen?

Danny scanned the room. Rug, bed, hula girl lamp, rotting banana peel, Lakers pennant, desk, brand-new, high-tech, adjustable height swivel chair . . . wait. The desk. It was neat. It was never neat. It had been especially not neat that afternoon when he had come in after school, thrown his books down, and left. Why was it neat now? Had very tidy Martians come in while he was playing basketball and cleaned up? Naw, Mom must have done that, Danny thought, looking at the detestable neatness she always managed to make out of his messy desk things without even asking permission first.

Oh well, house noises, Danny decided. Yeah, the noises he'd heard before must have just been some of those house noises, those little noises houses are always making that everyone is usually too busy to hear. Disappointed that no Martian monster-dog, or any other catastrophe for that matter, was going to save him from his homework, Danny walked over to his desk and sat down.

"Errrr."

That sound again.

"Woof!"

No house had ever made a noise like that before,

and as his whole class had reminded Danny that afternoon, he didn't *have* a dog.

"Woof, woof, woof, ERRRRRRR!"

Then it was on him!

"Don't make me be Martian dog food!" Danny screamed.

A shaggy tan and black dog with one long, bushy, black eyebrow was jumping on Danny, barking, wagging his tail, and licking Danny's ears. Every once in awhile the dog would do a little turn in midair. If this was a Martian monster-dog, he was certainly a friendly one. Danny was getting pretty soggy.

"Yuck!" Danny said. He laughed and wiped dog-slobber off his ears. "Whoa, boy! Where'd you come from?" Danny tried to pat the jumping dog.

"From over in the corner!" the dog replied. He couldn't get the words out fast enough. He jumped up and down a few more times and ran over to the corner of the room under the windows to show Danny the exact spot where he had been waiting.

Danny stopped laughing. He stopped moving. For a split second, he even stopped growing.

"What?" Danny asked softly.

"The corner, the corner!" the dog repeated, and spun around. "I thought you'd never come upstairs. Was dinner good?"

"Ooey kaflooey kachoo, kachoo, ooey kaflooey kalooey magooey mahooey manooey kachoo, kachoo, kaflooey, kafloo . . ." Danny mumbled his magic words softly to himself, over and over, faster and faster.

The dog stopped running and spinning and jumping and came over to Danny. His sad-looking beagle's eyes got even sadder, the way they always did when he was worried about someone. They drooped even lower than usual at the corners, and his bushy V-shaped eyebrow turned itself upside down, so that it looked less like a V, and more like a small thatched roof for his face.

"Are you all right, Danny?" the dog asked, and put a shaggy paw on Danny's knee.

After a couple of minutes Danny stopped saying his magic words. He finally realized that either they had worked, or the dog had never intended to gobble him down in the first place.

Danny looked at the dog and the dog looked at Danny.

"WEL-COME TO EARTH!" Danny said to the dog, very slowly and loudly, the way people sometimes talk to foreigners or people who can't hear very well.

The dog looked at Danny strangely.

"YOU SPEAK ENG-LISH VE-RY WELL!" Danny continued.

"Thanks a lot!" said the dog excitedly, and jumped around the room some more. He jumped around a lot when he was excited, as if he'd eaten a box of firecrackers once, and whenever he got excited, somehow a few of them had to go off. One second he'd be on the ground, and the next second he'd be in the air. He didn't seem to need a running start or anything. Danny couldn't figure out how he did it.

"See, you don't understand barking, so I have to talk to you with people-words," the dog explained while he jumped on the bed.

"Uh-huh." Danny nodded casually, as if he met talking Martian dogs every night after dinner.

Just then, Mom walked in. She never *could* learn to knock, no matter how many times Danny asked her.

Danny took in the situation instantly. He had seen enough movies to know what grown-ups did to cute little Martians. They turned them over to the police who gave them to scalpel-happy scientists who didn't just give them a talking-to that *felt* like a dissection; they *really dissected* them, or otherwise kept them from returning to the mother ship. And even though Mom was a fairly nice grown-up, she was still a grown-up, and would have to be true to her own kind. The dog must be kept a secret, that seemed perfectly clear.

Danny would have to get Mom out of the room as quickly as possible. He started to go to her, but she had a head start on him, and was at his desk before he could even stand up. At least her back was to the bed, where the dog was sitting still for a change. He twitched his eyebrow from time to time, but otherwise he was completely still.

He must sense the danger, Danny thought.

"I just came up to see if you needed some help," Mom said.

Danny grabbed a book, opened it, and instantly became the picture of a perfect student.

"Doing fine, Mom, just fine. Don't need any help. No help at all," he said. He got up and tried to steer her out of the room.

"Let's just *see* how you're doing," Mom said, placing her hand on his shoulder and easing him back into his seat.

"I told you, Mom, I'm doing fi—"

She was reaching for some papers that were piled up next to his books. He hadn't noticed those before. She picked the top paper.

"Let's see," she said, and started reading the paper out loud. " 'Danny Wilder, English, Chapter 11—Exercises.' " She scanned the page. "This looks good, honey." She sounded as if she were afraid to believe it. "This looks very good."

Danny was sure she had finally lost her mind. All mothers were a little off, but now his had gone right over the edge.

He grabbed the paper from her. The exercises were there, with every part of speech in place. If she was crazy, he was too.

Meanwhile, Mom had taken the next paper from the pile. " 'Danny Wilder, A Report on The Oregon Trail,' " she read. " 'The Oregon Trail was the main route traveled by wagon trains carrying settlers to Oregon. The trail was rugged and rough. The settlers faced many hardships.' " Mom skimmed the page. "Uh-huh . . . uh-huh . . . hunh. Interesting," she said to Danny. "People sacrificed a lot, didn't they?"

Mom put the paper down and Danny grabbed it. Mom was right. Just like the English homework, the Oregon Trail paper was done too, and it looked pretty good except that the starting point had been left blank. The paper read, "The starting point was. . . ." and then there was a space. Mom hadn't noticed that.

What's going on? thought Danny. He reached for the rest of the papers. Everything was there. Everything he needed to get done that night. The week's spelling list was there, copied out five times, and all of the next day's math problems. Even the book report on Wilt Chamberlain's biography, which he'd been putting off for a month, was in the pile, neatly printed out.

Danny knew he was getting away with something, but he had no idea how he'd done it. He decided not to worry about it. With a sigh, he leaned back in his chair and stretched.

"I'm all done, Mom," Danny said. "That talking-to did me a lot of good."

What a life, Danny thought, then out of the corner of his eye, he saw the dog. The dog! There he was, still sitting on the bed. Danny had no idea how much longer that would last. From the short time he'd known him, Danny could tell the dog was a jumpy, talkative one. No telling when he'd start up again.

Danny stood up. "Why don't you go downstairs and relax," he said to Mom casually, as he tried once more to steer her toward the door.

Then the dog, with a running leap that got him from the bed to the desk in a great furry blur, jumped on Danny and yelled, "*I* did your *homework! I* did your *homework! I* did your *homework!*" He almost knocked Danny down. Evidently, the dog had waited as long as he could, and then one of those firecrackers inside him just had to go off.

Danny stared at Mom, grinning idiotically. The dog was jumping around the room singing to himself. "*I* did Danny's *homework, I* did Danny's *homework!*"

"Danny, I'm very proud of you," Mom said. "See what you can accomplish when you really try?"

Why didn't she say something about the dog? Danny thought. He just kept staring at her, grinning.

"But I'm a little upset with you," Mom continued.

Here it comes, Danny thought. She'd been pretending not to see the dog to torture him, because she was still mad at him from before.

"You shouldn't play mean jokes like that on Daddy and me. Letting us lecture you like that when your homework was already done."

This was getting to be too much. "I wanted to surprise you," Danny said, still grinning. His face felt like it would break, he was grinning so hard. He couldn't take it anymore.

"*STOP IT!*" Danny screamed. "*I KNOW YOU SEE HIM!*" Danny leaped for the dog and hugged him.

"She can't see me," the dog said.

"*WHAT!?!*" yelled Danny.

"Danny, is something wrong?" asked Mom.

"She can't. See me that is," the dog said to Danny. "Or hear me."

"*Now* you tell me," Danny whispered.

Mom stared at Danny. "Tell you what?" she asked.

"Umm, ummm . . . I mean, '*I* tell *you!*' " Danny said to Mom. "I mean, 'I *should* have told you.' "

"Told me what?" Mom asked, confused.

"Told you it was all done. My homework, I mean." With that, Danny took Mom's arm and finally succeeded in steering her toward the door. She was almost out of the room when she turned suddenly and looked at Danny with a hard, penetrating gaze.

"Danny, are you planning some kind of a, a . . . trick or something?" Mom asked, more like a detective than a mother.

"Of course not, Mom, not me," Danny answered. How could she know? How could she possibly know? Mothers must have some kind of special radar for stuff like this.

Mom continued to stare at Danny, as if she looked at him long enough and hard enough his secret thoughts would tumble right out of his mouth, neatly printed on a computer printout sheet. Finally, she laughed. "Oh, Danny. I guess this is why I love you so much. You're a nut!" she said. "Now, I'm very pleased with the job you did tonight, but I want you to be sure this diligence continues." She gave Danny a kiss on the forehead, but Danny was so dazed by the evening's events that he forgot to protest.

"Why don't you come downstairs, honey?" Mom asked.

"In a few minutes, Mom."

Mom walked to the door.

"Just want to double-check some of those math problems," Danny added. Boy, was he milking it.

Mom beamed Danny one of her great you-really-are-the-best-son-in-the-world smiles and left.

Danny turned to the dog.

6

Homework

*F*inally alone in his room with the dog, Danny couldn't ask him questions fast enough. "What else can you do?" Danny asked. "Can you leap tall buildings in a single bound? Can you? Can you? That would be so incredible!"

"No," said the dog. "Sorry."

"Well I bet you're faster than a speeding bullet, and you can climb walls like a spider, and you can stretch yourself halfway around the world, and of course you have X-ray vision, and X-ray hearing, and X-ray sensory perception, and—"

"I'm afraid I can't do any of those things," said the dog. "Sorry."

"Oh," said Danny, a little disappointed.

"But I can leap and hover!" the dog said brightly.

"Leap and hover?" Danny asked.

"Yeah!" The dog was getting excited again. "Look!" He leaped from the bed up to the ceiling, stayed there for a minute, then floated gently back down to the bed.

"Like a helicopter!" Danny said. "Neat!"

"It helps me out in all sorts of ways," the dog said proudly. "It comes in very handy when a stick gets caught in a tree, and of course, it's how I got in here."

"But if you can do that, why can't you fly?"

The dog seemed embarrassed. "I simply don't have the right aerodynamics," he said sadly. "I tried to learn, I really did try, but I just couldn't get it."

"It's OK," Danny said, patting the dog. "I don't know any other dogs who can talk and do homework. By the way, thanks a lot for doing mine. You really got me off the hook tonight."

"No problem," said the dog.

"It looked very neat. Ms. McCardle will like that, she likes neatness. But you know, I think you forgot to put in the starting point of the Oregon Trail. I mean, you didn't get it wrong or anything, you just left it blank."

"Did I?" Homework asked, putting what he thought was a terribly innocent expression on his face. Danny showed him the paper.

"I guess I forgot," lied Homework. Of course he hadn't really forgotten. He was doing exactly what Ms. McCardle told him to do. He had left out the

starting place of the Oregon Trail on purpose. It
was all part of the *Plan for the Improving of Homework,* involving the boy while building self-esteem.
"Oh well, let's look it up together!" said Homework,
a phony smile pasted on his furry face.

A bell started to ring in Danny's head, softly at
first, then louder and louder, an alarm bell that
sounded anytime someone tried to get him to do
something he didn't want to do. In fact, the whole
situation was beginning to feel like just another
WARP. Danny looked Homework over carefully.

"By the way, what's your name?" the boy asked
the dog.

"Homework," said Homework.

"Homework. Of course," said Danny. "Homework, how'd you get so smart?"

"Have you ever heard anyone say, 'My dog ate it'
when he or she didn't have his or her homework?"
asked the dog.

Danny suffered a sudden coughing and gagging
fit. "I, I, uh, I think . . . so," he stammered.

"Well . . . I'm that dog!" Homework explained. "I
ate so much homework that I got very smart!"

Was this a joke? Was someone trying to get back
at him? For what? All he'd done was give some
stupid excuse to Ms. McCardle when he hadn't had
his homework. "Of course," Danny said, as if the
dog made perfect sense.

"That's why I don't eat very much," Homework explained. "Well, at least not food, anyway. You see, at this point in my evolution, the studying I do nourishes me, and I no longer actually have to eat the assignments. Of course, I always love a dog biscuit, and I'm crazy about oatmeal cookies."

"I'll try and get you some, sometime," Danny said, staring at the dog.

"Now, are you ready?" Homework asked.

"Ready for what?" asked Danny.

"The starting place of the Oregon Trail. Remember, we were going to look it up!" Homework put his front paws on Danny's social studies book and pushed it over to him.

Danny glared at the dog. The alarm bell inside Danny's head was ringing loud and clear now.

"Why me?" he asked the dog.

"Why you what?" the dog asked back.

"Why are you helping *me*? As opposed to some other kid."

"Oh, well, . . . umm, umm . . . I'm not really allowed to say exactly." Pause. One of Ms. McCardle's rules was that he could never say who sent him, or why. Homework hated secrets. "A friend sent me," he blurted out. "Yes, yes, definitely a friend."

Some friend, Danny thought. The dog was trying to trick him into doing homework. Who was this dog, really? Why was he here? What did it all mean?

"Can't find it?" Homework asked.

Danny realized that he had been looking down, in the direction of the social studies book the dog had pushed in front of him. He hadn't actually focused on anything on the page, but to the dog, it must have looked like he was studying. Danny looked at Homework blankly.

The black eyebrow on Homework's beagle face went up and down, up and down, up and down, as it always did when he was thinking hard. Homework looked at Danny and he looked at the social studies book. Finally, he rested his right paw on a map of the Oregon Trail. Next to his paw there was a star.

"Oh, I see," Danny said in a complete monotone. "The starting place was Independence, Missouri."

"Independence! Independence! Independence!" Homework repeated ecstatically. He leaped up to the ceiling and hovered there for a moment. "Independence is a *GREAT* name, isn't it? *Isn't it GREAT!?!*" he shouted as he floated down. "Don't you feel *GREAT* now!?!"

Great? Not great at all, but what? Danny asked himself.

He sat down on his bed and tried to straighten out the evening's events. But they wouldn't get straight.

First, I got grounded, Danny thought. That's

bad. Then, a magical homework dog did my home-work for me. That's fantastic! Or is it? The dog is amazing, but he tried to trick me into looking up the starting point of the Oregon Trail, which is awful. On the other hand, Mom and Dad are off my back for the night, so that's great. Except now, with my homework done, I'll do great in school tomorrow. That's no good. I'm trying *so* hard to flunk. OK, I won't hand the homework in. But then I'll get grounded again. Which will start the whole thing all over.

Danny sighed a weary sigh and stretched his arms high over his head.

Maybe living *WARP-FREE* is more trouble than it's worth, he thought. Maybe it's not even possible. After all, there's always *something* you have to do. Maybe I should just give up and *WARP* ahead like everyone else. Maybe . . .

Meanwhile, Homework had been waiting, some-thing he wasn't very good at. He'd worked his eye-brow up and down, up and down, up and down about a million times while he watched Danny, straining to figure out what the boy was thinking. Suddenly, the dog couldn't take any more. He jumped on to Danny's lap and stuck his face right up close to Danny's. "I bet we'll have even more fun doing your homework tomorrow!" he exclaimed.

"I don't think so," Danny said. "It was very nice

of you to help me tonight, but I'm afraid this isn't going to work ou—" Danny stopped in the middle of his sentence and stared at the dog. "Wait a minute. Did you say *tomorrow?*" Danny asked.

"Yes, tomorrow," said Homework, hopping off Danny's lap and onto the bed.

"And what about the day after that?" Danny asked.

"Yes," said the dog. "I'll help you then too."

"Just like tonight?"

"Just like tonight."

"Exactly how *long* are you planning on *staying?*" Danny asked the dog.

"As long as necessary," answered Homework.

"As long as necessary?" Danny asked.

"Yes, as long as necessary," the dog repeated.

This is *it!* Danny thought. The dog was the answer!

Danny's thoughts went faster and faster, as he calculated the incredible beauty of his situation.

Mom and Dad said I would be grounded "*as long as necessary,*" Danny thought. Now this dog comes along and says he's going to help me "*as long as necessary!*" That's the same amount of time! Which means that as long as I don't do my homework, it will be *necessary* for the dog to stay and do it *for* me. He seems like a nice dog. He wouldn't want me to be grounded.

"Do you want me to be grounded?" Danny asked Homework.

"Of course not," Homework answered. "I'm here to help!"

Yes! Danny thought. Finish fifth grade and on to middle school *WARP-FREE* with a homework dog! High school and college? Easy. I'll study when I feel like it, after all, some of the courses might be interesting, but I'll be able to goof off whenever I'm in the mood! No test schedules to worry about. No due dates to hang me up. I'll be on my own, in control! Hey, maybe after college, Homework will even go to work for me! *You can't catch me, 'cuz I'm WARP-WARP-WARP-FREE!*

"You really mean *as long as necessary!?!*" Danny asked the dog one more time, just to be doubly sure.

"As long as necessary!" Homework exclaimed.

"Great," Danny said. "That's just great."

"Great!" said Homework.

Danny smiled.

Homework smiled back, certain that the good feelings were already starting to take hold of Danny—he seemed so happy. Ms. McCardle would be so pleased, Homework thought.

"Can I get you an oatmeal cookie?" Danny asked, heading for the door.

Homework drooled appreciatively.

7

Throw, Miss

With Homework's trick of becoming invisible to anyone he didn't want to see him, he was able to go everywhere and do anything with Danny.

Starting the very next morning, Danny and Homework got up together and went to school. Homework trotted through the school doors at Danny's side and followed him into class, invisible to everyone except Danny, and of course, Ms. Mc-Cardle. Being Ms. McCardle's dog, Homework was always visible to her, but that was OK, since he was helping Danny at her request. In public situations she always pretended not to see him.

Danny sat down at his desk, then Homework leaped up to the exact height of Danny's desk chair and hovered there next to him, sort of sitting in midair. That way Homework didn't take up any desk space, which might have been inconvenient; he didn't have to sit on Danny's lap, which might have been uncomfortable; and he didn't need an extra chair placed next to Danny's desk, which might have attracted attention.

"What's that chair doing there?" someone might have asked. "It's blocking the aisle."

"My invisible, talking, Martian, homework dog is sitting there," Danny would have had to answer. Imagine how hard Tommy Lewis would have laughed then.

"Now you can really see the advantages of leaping and hovering," Homework said to Danny from his hover position.

"I still don't see why you can't fly," Danny whispered. "It seems like it would be so easy."

Homework just shrugged his shoulders.

All morning long, Homework helped Danny with class discussions and his schoolwork. Whenever Ms. McCardle called on Danny, Homework did his best.

"Danny, please correct this sentence," Ms. McCardle said after scrawling, "Louisa and me am playing basketball," across the blackboard.

Danny walked to the board with Homework right behind him. Homework leaped and hovered in front of the sentence.

"What do you think is wrong with the sentence?" Homework whispered.

Danny gave him a blank look.

"Go ahead, Danny," Ms. McCardle said, with a sly wink at Homework.

A few kids in the class started to giggle.

"Louisa and *I are* playing basketball," Homework whispered to Danny, and Danny wrote it on the board.

"Very good, Danny," Ms. McCardle said.

The giggling stopped.

"Very good," she said again later, when Homework told Danny and Danny told the class the correct answer to a particularly difficult problem in long division with decimals.

Homework helped Danny all day long. Occasionally Homework gave Danny the wrong answer on purpose, for two reasons: one—to see if he could or would correct the mistake, and two—so that Danny's grades wouldn't rise above his former grade level—*B*'s with a few *A*'s. Strictly according to the *Plan*.

At the end of the school day, Homework couldn't wait to get home. True, Danny hadn't helped with a single question all day, but, we're only just beginning, Homework reassured himself.

"Come on! Come on!" the dog called to the boy, racing up the stairs to Danny's room that afternoon. "Watch this! Watch this!" Homework shouted, jumping on Danny's bed.

Danny strolled into the room and shut the door.

Homework leaped up to Danny's desk and sat very still. He drew three circles in the air, much the same way Ms. McCardle did when she used her red-enameled apple, and chanted softly:

"Flash cards, flash cards,
East, West, North, South,
Flash cards, flash cards,
Hasten hither—
To my mouth!"

He opened his mouth wide, as if he were going to yawn, and about thirty flash cards materialized in the four corners of the room and flew into his mouth. He put them down on the desk with a flourish.

"Check out these flash cards!" Homework said. "You'll ace 'em."

"Fantastic trick!" Danny said.

"You *bet* it is!" Homework chimed. "But what's more fantastic are these math problems!" Homework smiled his toothiest smile and gently pushed a flash card in Danny's direction.

"Sorry, I don't, uh . . . err . . . believe in flash cards," Danny said. "But you go right ahead, Homework."

Then, instead of sitting down and doing flash cards with Homework, the way most kids would have, Danny started bustling around the room. He took a hanger out of his closet and fashioned a hoop out of it. Then he took some string, a pair of scissors, and a roll of tape from his desk. He cut about twenty ten-inch lengths of string, and tied these onto the hanger hoop, hanging them all around, twisting and knotting them to make a sort of net. When that was done, he bent the hook of the hanger up at a right angle to the hoop and taped the thing to his bedroom door.

"What do you think?" Danny asked Homework.

"Very creative," Homework said, "but how will this help you with flash cards?"

Danny laughed and went to his desk where he got a stack of about thirty sheets of notebook paper. He took them over to his bed, plumped the pillows, leaned back, crumpled up a sheet of paper, and tossed it through the hoop.

Throw, miss.

He crumpled another sheet.

Throw, whoosh. Basket.

"*Yes!*" said Danny.

Throw, miss.

For a minute or two, Homework's mouth hung open and his head moved gently from side to side as he traced the arc each shot made soaring across the room. But that didn't last long.

"How can anyone not believe in *flash cards?*"

Homework asked, snapping back into action. "They're *fun!* They incorporate the competitive spirit of the sports arena into the learning process!"

Homework looked like a cheerleader. He balanced on his hind legs and waved his front paws in the air.

"Sorry. I guess they're sort of fun," Danny said, "but this is more fun. This isn't *like* sports, it *is* sports."

Throw, miss.

"Rats," Danny muttered.

"Rats," Homework muttered.

"What's wrong?" Danny asked. "You didn't miss a basket."

"Oh, it's this problem," Homework answered, pointing to one of the flash cards. "I just can't seem to get it. Give me a hand with it, won't you?"

"Give me a break, Homework. You know everything about everything. Stop faking it," Danny said.

"What do you mean?" Homework asked, his most innocent expression pasted on his furry face.

Danny laughed and shot another basket.

"OK, OK," Homework said. "You don't believe in flash cards? That's OK. Everyone is entitled to their not-to-beliefs. But look at this—this is *really* going to get you!"

Homework fumbled around on the desk and

opened a magazine to an article that Danny was supposed to read for social studies.

"The Electoral College!" Homework exclaimed. "Why this is more fun than the circus! What a *hoot!* Sounds like a real college, right? Right? [herr, herr, harr] Where people go to learn how to get elected or something, right? [harr, harr, herr] Well . . . it's not!!! [HARR!] What crazy guys our founding fathers were, huh? What jokers! Now, for every statement you contribute to this discussion, you get a sticker!"

Homework circled his paw in the air three times and started to chant:

> "Stickers, stickers,
> East, West, North, South,
> Stickers, stickers,
> Hasten hither,
> To my—"

Danny cut him short. "Don't they get stuck on your tongue?" he asked. "Anyway, stickers are for fourth graders. No thanks."

Throw, whoosh. Basket.

Homework looked at Danny and smiled. "You will help out later, won't you?" he asked.

"Sure, sure," Danny answered, crumpling up another sheet of paper.

Homework grasped a pencil tightly between his two front paws and started doing the night's assignments. Tomorrow will be better, he reassured himself. It's only the first day.

"How are you doing, Danny?" Grandma hollered up the stairs. She was babysitting for the afternoon, in spite of all of Danny's protests to his parents. "Need any help?" Grandma asked.

"No thanks, Grandma, I'm doin' fine," Danny hollered back. "I should be done in no time." Danny glanced over his shoulder at his desk and saw Homework, hard at work. "I have an interesting new study aid!" he called down to Grandma.

At the end of the afternoon, Danny showed Grandma his completed assignments, and she crossed them off the bulletin board in the kitchen.

"Very good, Danny," Grandma said.

The next day, Homework was his most encouraging, helpful self with Danny at school, but still, Danny did not help answer a single question, or volunteer a single comment of his own for class discussions. The boy was very cooperative whenever Homework told him what to do or what to say, but did absolutely nothing on his own.

Home will be better, Homework thought. It's only the second day.

That afternoon at home, Homework decided to try flattery with Danny. *"Flattery will get you every-*

where," he seemed to remember Ms. McCardle saying.

"You know you're really very smart!" Homework said to Danny, in Danny's room after school. "You said a very smart thing just before you lay down on your bed and started shooting those baskets! You said, *'That snack was good.' 'That snack was good,'* that was *really smart,* you know?" Then Homework circled his paw three times and recited one of his magic chants. A diagram of a baseball field with a sentence to correct positioned at each base materialized on Danny's desk.

"Flattery will get you nowhere," said Danny.

Throw, whoosh. Basket.

"No, you've got it wrong," said Homework. "Flattery will get you *everywhere.*"

Danny laughed gently and shot another basket.

"Does this mean you're not helping again?" asked Homework.

"Right," said Danny.

"Tomorrow you will, right?"

"Sure, sure," Danny answered.

"Need any help?" Grandma hollered up the stairs.

"Doin' fine, Grandma," Danny yelled down.

Throw, whoosh. Basket.

Homework sat down and did Danny's assignments.

None of the assignments I've done for him have come back yet, Homework told himself. Once they do, the good feelings from all those *B*'s with a few *A*'s will just bowl Danny over!

Homework didn't have to wait long. The very next day at school, Ms. McCardle handed back the assignments from the last two days. That afternoon at home, Homework spread them out all over Danny's bed. Most of them had big *B*'s marked in red at the top, a few had *A*'s.

"Pretty great, don't ya think, buddy?" Homework said.

"Yeah, yeah. Thanks a lot," Danny said.

Whoosh. The baskets started.

"Great!" Homework exclaimed. "Now let's go!"

"You go ahead."

"But I thought the grades made you feel great."

"They're OK."

"But you still don't feel like helping?"

"Tomorrow I will."

Grandma hollered up the stairs. "I know you probably don't need any help, Danny, but your mom just called and asked me to ask you!"

"Doin' fine Grandma!" Danny called down the stairs.

"Doin' fine," Grandma said downstairs on the phone to Mom.

Doin' fine? Homework wondered as he started

working on the day's assignments. Not fine at all, he told himself, but then, it's only the third day.

So it went. For two weeks the dog was his most enthusiastic, flattering, gung-ho self. He made every study aid he could think of materialize in Danny's room. There were games: mazes, matching games, unmatching games, medieval castle games, miniature football games with questions every ten yards, and games with animated hologram monsters. There were presentations: he showed 3-D movies (with the customary 3-D glasses), he recited epic poems he had written himself, he told stories, he wrote and performed zippy little songs on pertinent topics, he even did a one-dog show where he acted out all the major battles of the Civil War, but after two weeks, Danny still had not answered a single question in class or helped with a single aspect of any homework assignment.

For two weeks Homework kept telling himself that tomorrow would be better, but it never was. According to the *Plan,* he was supposed to spend three weeks with Danny before checking in with Ms. McCardle. By the afternoon of the last day of his second week with Danny, Homework knew he was running out of tomorrows.

Homework sat at Danny's desk, Danny's books open in front of him, but he couldn't concentrate. "*AOOOOOOOOOOOO!*" he howled.

Danny looked over at him from his usual position

on his bed and asked, "Is there a problem, little buddy?"

Homework jumped down from the desk and jumped up to Danny's bed. "You bet there's a problem!" he yelled. "You! You're the problem! I encourage, I flatter, I make fantastic stuff materialize just for you. I act out every major battle of the Civil War, and I still can't get you to help with anything!"

"But I don't understand," Danny said. "I thought you said you were going to help me as long as necessary."

"You mean it's still necessary?" Homework asked.

"Oh, yes, definitely," Danny answered.

"Why?" Homework asked.

"Well . . ." Danny stalled. "Because I just don't want . . . can't umm, umm . . ."

"Are you trying to tell me you don't have good feelings about yourself?" Homework asked, placing a sympathetic paw on Danny's knee.

"That's it," Danny said. "That's it exactly! How did you know?"

"I'm a dog," said Homework. "Dogs know about kids."

Homework climbed down from Danny's bed. He glanced up at the books on Danny's desk, but felt too upset to get anything done. Instead, he began pacing the floor.

The poor kid still doesn't feel good, Homework thought, working his eyebrow into a frenzy. The

Plan isn't working for him. I tried to tell Ms. Mc-Cardle the *Plan* is outdated, but she wouldn't listen. She wouldn't listen. She wouldn't . . .

"Better get busy, Homework, don't you think?" Danny said. "All this wandering around won't get the work done. How about knocking off a few *B*'s and an *A* before dinner, huh?"

Homework stopped dead in his tracks. "YA-HOO!!!" he shouted. He leaped up to the ceiling and floated gently down. "Thank you!!!"

"Any time," Danny said, looking a little puzzled.

That's what was wrong! Homework thought. Why hadn't he seen it before?

According to the *Plan*, Homework was supposed to get the student's grades back up to where they had been before the student started needing help. And that was exactly what Homework had done with Danny. But, *obviously*, "B's *and a few A's*" weren't enough for Danny! They didn't encourage enough good feelings in Danny to spur him on to getting involved.

Danny needs *straight A's!* Homework thought. He would update the *Plan*. He jumped to Danny's desk, whipped open Danny's English book, and started writing down answers so fast he looked more like a homework machine than a homework dog.

"That's more like it," said Danny.

I hope so, Homework thought. I surely hope so.

A Feeling of *A*'s

*H*omework kept working harder than ever and the *A*'s started pouring in. *A*'s at the top of each assignment Homework did for Danny. *A*, *A*, *A*. So many *A*'s, where before there had been just a few. This had never happened to Danny before. Half-way through fifth grade Danny became a horrible student. Before that he had been a good student. But *A*, *A*, *A*? Never. Suddenly, Danny started getting them in everything.

Grandma was usually the first one at home to see Danny's work. She was happy when she saw that Danny was doing his work again, but when the *A*'s started coming, she beamed.

"I always knew you had it in you," she said. "Straight *A*'s! Wow! I wish Grandpa Jack were alive to see this."

"Thank you, Grandma," Danny said.

Mom and Dad had been thrilled when Danny's grades improved to B's with a few A's, but when Danny started getting *straight* A's, they were ecstatic. Of course, they said all the regular parent stuff like, "Good work," and "We're proud," and, "Isn't that wonderful?" but mostly they looked at Danny in a goofy sort of way, and Mom's eyes got shiny.

Even Evie started to treat Danny with a little respect.

"You're very tall," she said one day, staring heavenward.

"Yes, I *am* tall, little sister," Danny answered, like a space hero about to invade a new galaxy. "You will be taller than you are now, one day, if you eat properly."

"When you finish your homework today, you can marry my Judy doll," Evie said. Then she gave Danny his future bride to hold for a minute.

"I'm truly honored," Danny said, trying not to gag as he looked at the doll's fluorescent, glow-in-the-dark, changeable-color hair that was bright purple at the moment.

Eric Bedemeyer was dumbfounded.

"Very impressive," he said to Danny one day at lunch. "Very impressive. Very impressive. Very impressive. Very im—"

"Thanks," said Danny. Then Eric gave Danny half of his Hostess Twinkie.

But the all-time best came a little more than two weeks after Homework had come to stay with Danny. Ms. McCardle held up an English paper Homework had written for Danny, in front of the whole class. Like all of his recent assignments, it was marked with a big red *A* at the top. Homework had called it "Spring," and the paper described how the playground was changing from a frozen wintery grayness into a pale green wonderland of grass and baseball and swing sets. Ms. McCardle read the whole thing out loud to the class, and no one even laughed. Well, only Tommy Lewis, but that was only for a second.

When school was over for the day, Francy Kloss came over to Danny and told him she thought the paper was beautiful. "Poetic," she had said. Yes, poetic was the word she had used as she shook her perm. Then she touched Danny's hand.

"*A*'s sure are nice," Danny called to Homework as the two walked home from school that day.

Homework, who had been straggling along behind, smelling every bush and tree they passed, shot to Danny's side. "They sure are, aren't they, aren't they, aren't they!" he chimed, more excited than Danny had ever seen him before.

It's working, it's working! Homework thought.

The good feelings are taking hold! *Straight A's!* I knew that was the ticket!

And just in time, too. Homework had been with Danny about two and a half weeks. If he was lucky, he'd be able to get Danny to do a little work on his own before he had to check in with Ms. Mc-Cardle at the three week point, according to the *Plan.*

Homework jumped in circles all around Danny. "Those *A*'s kind of give you a good feeling about yourself, don't they, don't they, don't they, buddy?" he chimed.

"Yep, they sure do," Danny answered, smiling. He rubbed his hand where Francy had touched it.

"GREAT! GREAT! GREAT!!!" Homework shouted, gloating.

That night, when Danny told his family that Ms. McCardle had read his paper to the class, they all insisted he read it to them, too. Grandma had stayed for supper, and Evie held Judy up so the doll could hear, too. Danny had a big audience. When he finished, they all sat and looked at him. No one made a sound, except for Mom, who was crying a little.

"I'm sorry, [sniff]" she said. "It was just so *beautiful.*" [She wiped her eyes on her napkin.] "It was really beautiful, honey." She hugged Danny.

"Nice work," Dad said, and hugged Danny too. "I

didn't know you could write like that. That was really something."

Evie pretended Judy was crying, too, and wiped the doll's eyes.

"I wish Grandpa Jack could've heard that," Grandma said.

"Thank you," Danny said.

"I don't think any parent grounds an *A* student, do you, honey?" Dad said to Mom.

"Of course not," Mom answered, smiling at Danny.

He looked at the people seated around him at the dining room table. His family. They were all looking at him. They all looked so proud. Then he looked down at the paper he had just read, that he knew he had not written. He had fooled them, fooled them all—his teacher, his friends, even his family. How fantastic! *You can't catch me, 'cuz I'.n WARP-FREE!* Weekend melted into weekday with no muss, no fuss, and things would continue this way, as Homework had promised. *"As long as necessary."* As long as he didn't do his homework, it would be *necessary* for the dog to stay and do it for him. Everything was perfect, absolutely perfect. Yet, suddenly, Danny had to get away.

"I gotta go," he mumbled. He fumbled clumsily with his chair and hurried up to his room.

"Isn't that something," Mom whispered to

Grandma and Dad. "What a change. And to think, just a few weeks ago, he couldn't even finish an assignment."

When Danny opened the door to his room, Homework was waiting for him, sure that the *A*'s had finally taken effect, sure that Danny would finally be able to study.

"Let's go, buddy!" he called. "Time to hit the books!"

"No," said Danny.

"What do you mean, no?" asked Homework.

"I mean, no."

"But I thought you felt good," Homework said. "I thought you liked that feeling of *A*'s."

"I don't," Danny said.

"You know," Homework said, "I've been very patient with you, but if you want me to keep helping you . . ."

"But I *don't* want you to keep helping me!" Danny snapped. "Not any more—I don't want *straight A's!* I don't want any *A*'s at all! When you get straight *A*'s, everyone pays attention! They share Twinkies with you, they give you dolls to marry, they cry!"

"Don't you like that?" Homework asked quietly. "Doesn't that make you feel good?"

"I *hate* it," Danny said. "It's creepy. You did that work, not me! You know that!"

"You could do terrific work on your own if you'd

just try!" Homework cried. "Try now! I'll help you!"

This seemed to catch Danny off guard.

"Let me help you," Homework pleaded.

Danny took a deep breath, then said, "I'm going to flunk. Please don't help me anymore." Danny walked out of the room.

Homework heard the front door slam. Soon after he heard the sound of a basketball hitting the driveway. Homework reached for Danny's English book, then dropped his paw. He reached for Danny's notebook, only to drop his paw again. *Straight A's*, he had thought. What a brilliant idea, he had thought. Now he sat at Danny's desk, looking from one textbook to the other, and knew that none of them held the answer to this question: How could he have been so wrong?

9

Confession

"*I*'ll confess. That's the only thing to do," Danny whispered to Homework the next morning at school. "I'll go to Ms. McCardle, and I'll tell her the whole thing, and I'll flunk. That's what I was going to do before you came, anyway." He patted Homework on the head. "Thank you for all your help, but please go away."

Homework stayed in his usual place, hovering next to Danny's desk.

"Oops, she's busy," Danny whispered to Homework. "She's talking to those kids there, see? I'll confess at lunch." Danny looked over at the dog. "You haven't left yet?" Danny whispered. The dog hadn't budged. "All right, stay," Danny whispered, "but don't help me with any more schoolwork."

Danny spent the rest of the day not participating in class discussions, not handing in his homework, not paying attention to anything except Ms. McCardle. He watched and waited for an opportunity to speak to her.

At lunch Ms. McCardle was in a hurry. Not a good time for a confession.

"After lunch," Danny whispered to Homework. After lunch Ms. McCardle was grading papers.

"This afternoon for sure," Danny told Homework. One o'clock. Time for math. Two o'clock. Out came the social studies books. Now he would tell her. He really would. Two thirty. The bell would ring in thirty minutes. He had to tell her before the bell rang. He couldn't stay after school to tell her because everyone would think he was a wimp. Only girls stayed after the three o'clock bell rang to talk to the teacher. Fair or unfair, there was some unwritten rule which did not allow boys to do that.

"I'm sure I don't have to remind any of you not to come to school on Monday," Danny heard Ms. McCardle say, and the kids laughed. "I want you all to have a good spring vacation. Your only assignment is your book report—I'll give you these last few minutes before the bell rings to get started."

"Spring vacation," Danny whispered to Homework. "Too bad I have to confess now. If I do, Ms.

McCardle will probably write another note home, which means I'll probably spend spring vacation being grounded."

All the kids started reading, except Danny. He watched Ms. McCardle as she walked up and down the aisles, stopping to speak privately to one kid, then another. Up one aisle, and down another, whisper-whisper, chat-chat. She would get to him in a matter of seconds, and then he would have to . . .

"Glad to see you doing such excellent work lately, Danny," Ms. McCardle said, bending over Danny's desk. Homework smiled a forced smile up at her from his hover position, but, as always when there were other people around, Ms. McCardle pretended not to see him, and spoke only to Danny. "I was wondering why you weren't participating today," Ms. McCardle went on. "Aren't you feeling well?"

"Actually, I . . . umm, I uh . . . wanted to talk to you about my doing so well lately, and why I didn't do so well today." Danny said.

"Yes?" Ms. McCardle looked straight at him and waited for him to continue.

He meant to tell her, he wanted to tell her, oh, well, he had better just blurt it out. *I'VE BEEN CHEATING BY LETTING A TALKING HOME-WORK DOG DO ALL OF MY ASSIGNMENTS FOR*

ME!" In his nervousness, Danny ended up speaking much louder than he had intended to speak. The whole class heard him. They were hysterical.

"*AOOOOOOOO!!!*" howled Tommy Lewis.

"*WOOF, WOOF, ROOOOF!*" barked the kids. They all laughed and pointed at Danny. It seemed to Danny that they had never laughed at him quite so hard.

Ms. McCardle clapped her hands together. "Class, class!" she shouted. "Stop this instantly!"

Still they kept barking, and howling, and panting around the room like they would never stop. Usually Danny enjoyed this kind of kidding around. Now he smiled so the kids wouldn't think they were bugging him, but the fact was that somehow, today, he just wasn't in the mood. The night before, his family had treated him like he was Mr. Perfect; now here he was, the class clown; and really, he wasn't either one of those things.

"Quiet now!" Ms. McCardle demanded, and the noise died down. "It seems Danny was just playing another of his little tricks on us," Ms. McCardle said, laughing lightly. "Of course there's no such thing as a homework dog. Now thank you, Danny, for giving us a good laugh. Everyone, please get back to your reading."

She waited a second for everyone to get busy again, then said softly to Danny, "Is there something you want to tell me? I want very much to help you."

Danny just shook his head.

"If someone has been helping you, or even doing work for you," Ms. McCardle said, shooting a split second kill-look at Homework, "maybe it's time to do some work on your own. Is that what's happened?"

Danny nodded.

"I know how capable you are. You just have to jump in and do it." Ms. McCardle started to move away from Danny's desk, then turned to Homework, and in a loud stage whisper said, "After school. Today." She practically hissed.

"What, Ms. McCardle?" Danny asked.

Ms. McCardle was instant composure. "Nothing, nothing, just thinking out loud," she said brightly. "Reminding myself to stop at the cleaner's after school today."

Just then, about ten to three, the principal of the school walked into the room and coughed. He could never just say hello like a normal person, no, he always had to enter and cough, then look up expectantly and wait for someone to notice him.

"Hello, Mr. Jessup," Ms. McCardle said and walked to the front of the room. "Class, Mr. Jessup has something very important to tell us," she announced.

The kids stared at their principal with a glazed, vacant look.

"Hello, children," Mr. Jessup said. Mr. Jessup evidently did not know that one should never say, "Hello, children," to fifth graders. One should simply say, "Hello." The kids' eyes got their second and third coats of glaze.

"Well, children, [would he ever learn?] before you start your spring vacation I'd like to remind you that the Great Think-Off Contest is only two months away." He had one of those thin, colorless voices that isn't quite high, and isn't quite low, either; it's just sort of there, being annoying.

Mr. Jessup pointed to the empty sign-up sheet on the bulletin board and tapped quickly several times.

"If we get organized now, I know we can do a *fine job*, a *fine job!*" he said. "But I must say, I'm disappointed. In two months, fifth graders from all over the city will proudly represent their schools at the contest, and look at this." He pointed again to the empty sign-up sheet. "Will we have no team from our own dear school, our very own Lewis and Clark?" He waited for a response. There was none. "We can't let those Westside kids walk away with all the awards again, can we?" Mr. Jessup asked, and laughed heartily. At what, no one knew. He droned on, "You know, this contest has been held annually for ten years now, and I'm very sad to say that Lewis and Clark has never won."

"In fact, we've always lost!" That was Tommy Lewis, of course. All the kids laughed while Mr. Jessup had a small coughing fit.

"That's not true," Mr. Jessup said nervously. "One year we didn't lose."

Tommy Lewis called out again, "That's because the bus broke down and our kids never even *got* to the contest!"

The kids went nuts. Ms. McCardle aimed one of her kill-looks at them, and they laughed a little bit softer, but not much.

Mr. Jessup managed to raise his nothing-voice over the din. "I've arranged for a practice match, with our soon-to-be-formed Lewis and Clark team pitted against the Westside scholars, to be held in our auditorium the first Friday after vacation, and I want to see some names appear on this list right now." Silence. "Come children!" That word again. "Let's get our vacation off to a good start. I'm counting on this class, since [cough, cough] it's the best in the school." He smiled broadly.

"You mean you couldn't *get* anyone from the other fifth-grade classes to do it!" Tommy Lewis yelled out.

"Tommy Lewis, you will please do two book reports over vacation instead of only one," said Ms. McCardle.

At that moment, a roomful of mummies would have had more life in it than Ms. McCardle's fifth-grade classroom. All the kids looked like they'd been in tombs for thousands of years, that is, everyone except Danny. Danny was smiling broadly, as if someone had just told him a marvelous joke. It would be so *easy*, he thought, so *incredibly easy! Who could resist?* Danny looked over at Homework and pictured the whole thing—himself at the contest, with Homework hovering by his side, feeding him answers to question after question.

Mr. Jessup tapped the sign-up sheet again. *Tap-tap-tap-tap-tap.* "Right *now*, I said." Mr. Jessup coughed. He turned to Ms. McCardle. "Perhaps we had better just pick some children to *volunteer*," he said. Mr. Jessup was very proud of his knowledge of child psychology. He pretended to be looking the class over, sure that his act would get lots of kids to sign up.

"I take it all back," Danny whispered to Homework. "Don't go away. I still want you to help me."

"What?" said Homework.

Danny didn't hear him. He raised his hand.

"Yes?" said Mr. Jessup. "Do you want to sign up?"

"First I have to know if the contest is extracurricular," Danny said.

"Yes, it is," said Mr. Jessup.

"That means no credit, right?" Danny asked.

"There is so much besides *credit* to be gained from

extracur—" Mr. Jessup answered in his roundabout way, until Ms. McCardle interrupted.

"Right. No credit," she said.

"Then I'll sign up!" Danny said. He walked to the front of the room and signed his name on the sign-up sheet.

This is *perfect*, Danny thought, absolutely *perfect*. It's *extracurricular!* No credit! I can *win* the contest, and still *flunk!* That way, when I do flunk, everyone will know it's because I *wanted* to, not because I'm some kind of clown who can't even pass.

Mr. Jessup beamed. "Now that's what I call school spirit!" he said as loudly as his nothing-voice would allow. "Anyone else?" He kept tapping the sign-up sheet. "No one else?"

Ms. McCardle smiled at Danny, then tried to get Homework's attention. Homework made a point of looking out the window at that moment.

A low murmuring started coming from the kids. The bell rang, and the murmuring turned into talking. Everyone was talking about Danny.

Francy Kloss said to her friend Sue Zimmer, "I think he's very brave."

Martha Coffin, who was usually so serious and gloomy she looked like she should be in a coffin instead of named one, said, "Well. Well, well, well."

Tommy Lewis came over to Danny and in a phoney-polite voice asked, "Is your talking homework dog coming with you to give you all the answers at the contest?"

"Absolutely," Danny answered, deadly serious.

Tommy just laughed, then, faking hysteria and panic, he whined, "Sorry, uh . . . I don't know the answer to that one, my dog ate it . . . my . . . uh, my elephant stepped on it, my . . . my . . . my boa constrictor strangled it!" He clutched his throat and wiggled around violently, pretending he was being strangled—"Agh, ugh, ugh, yugh!"

Eric Bedemeyer walked up to Danny at the front of the room. "Have you completely lost your mind?" he whispered.

"What do you mean, 'Have I lost my mind?' " Danny asked.

"Be real, Danny," Eric said. "A few weeks ago you were flunking every subject."

"I can do it," Danny said. "You'll see—I have a secret weapon." Danny looked over at Homework and smiled, but, of course, Eric couldn't see Homework and didn't know what Danny was talking about. "In fact, I say let's go get a soda to celebrate!" Danny went on. "My certain victory, that is. Also, I'm not grounded anymore. For now, anyway."

Eric still worried. "Danny, these Westside kids *study*. I mean they *really study*."

"I'll be fine. Don't worry," Danny said.

The two boys left the classroom together. Homework tried sneaking out after them, but stopped dead at the door when he felt Ms. McCardle staring at him with no ordinary kill-look. No, it was a terminator-laser-annihilation-look which practically penetrated his fur with its lethal heat. Homework had no choice. He slunk over to Ms. McCardle's desk.

CHAPTER

10

Meeting the Enemy

"**W**ould you *MIND* telling me what is *GOING ON* here?" Ms. McCardle stormed at Homework, but she didn't give him a chance to answer. "Let's forget for a moment that Danny just signed up for a contest that he probably thinks you're going to win for him, and that you will of course tell him you have no intention of winning for him, and let me ask you, have you been getting straight *A*'s *for* Danny, or has Danny been *helping with the work?*"

"Arf," Homework said, hanging his head.

"Not at all?"

"Arf bark."

"Homework, this is terrible! You and I both know that according to *Plan* policy, you were only supposed to get Danny's grades up to his previous level! Of course, had he started working independently, it would have been appropriate for you to encourage him to work to his full potential. But now! Getting straight A's without any involvement on Danny's part—this might be catastrophic! Danny is obviously uncomfortable with the whole situation, he—"

Homework interrupted. He couldn't take any more. *"ARF ARF WOOF WOOF, AOOO! ARF ARF WOW WOW BOW BOW, BARK ARF ERF! AOOOOOO!"*

"How can you *say* that?" stormed Ms. McCardle. "The *Plan* works! It's *always* worked!"

"Bark bark bow wow!" snapped Homework, then he started to tell Ms. McCardle about the impossibility of getting Danny to do anything other than shoot baskets.

Before he'd gotten very far, he and Ms. McCardle heard footsteps in the hall, running footsteps, running fast.

"We *must* discuss this further," Ms. McCardle whispered frantically. "Meet me to—"

She never finished her sentence. Before she could, Danny ran into the room, panic-stricken. He'd taken his time, chatting and joking around in the hallway leaving school, and had finally noticed Homework was missing just as he'd closed the school doors behind him. He'd looked around outside. He'd thrown the doors open and looked down the hall. No Homework. Racing back to Ms. Mc-Cardle's room, he'd searched frantically for Homework along the way. No dog. Finally, back at Ms. McCardle's room, he ran in, and there was Homework. And there was Ms. McCardle, staring at Danny as if he had grown antlers and three heads.

In his best Mr. Cool voice, Danny said, "Oh, gee, Ms. McCardle, I guess I forgot a book." He went to his desk and took out a book he didn't really need. "Oh, here it is," he said. "Guess I'll just be *going now*," he added, staring right at Homework, and jerking his head toward the door, hoping Homework would get the hint.

Ms. McCardle pretended to busy herself with the papers on her desk.

Eric showed up. "Here you are," he said to Danny. "Boy, you really took off."

"We're . . . I mean, *I'm* coming now," Danny said, giving Homework another pointed look.

As the boys started to leave the classroom, Danny kept looking back every other step or so to make sure Homework was with them.

They had just stepped out the door of the classroom, when Ms. McCardle whispered to Homework, "Tonight!"

Danny heard her. He turned around and looked at her from the doorway. "Did you say something, Ms. McCardle? Something about tuna?"

For a split second, Ms. McCardle was thrown.

But she was a pro, and she recovered fast. "Oh, oh, just talking to myself—going to have *tuna* for dinner *tonight*. I like *tuna*, don't you?"

"Sure," said Danny giving her a strange look. "Tuna's nice."

"I like to have it late at night, for a snack sometimes," Ms. McCardle explained, then added pointedly, "when everyone is asleep."

"Right," Danny said with a bewildered look on his face. "Tuna. Great snack. Now I guess I'll just be going." He caught Homework's eye and motioned toward the door a couple of times with his head.

"Tuna," Ms. McCardle repeated as Homework left with the boys.

The neighborhood McDonald's was crowded that afternoon. It had been a very hot day, as if a summer day had gotten confused with an early spring day and come too early, zooming the thermometers up to seventy. Everyone was thirsty, and besides, spring vacation had begun. The place was jammed.

Danny, Eric, and Homework entered. Eric ordered a Coke, Danny ordered a milk shake for himself, and a glass of water and a package of oatmeal cookies, Homework's favorite. They sat down. Danny took a sip of the shake and opened the package of cookies. Then, when no one was looking, he leaned over and put them and the glass of water on the floor for Homework.

"Hey, don't scare me like that again," Danny whispered to Homework. "For a second I thought you were gone for good. That would be a total disaster—right after I signed up for that contest! Which we'll ace, by the way. Good dog. Now, eat your cookies." He gave the dog a pat and sat up.

All around them, kids were enjoying cool drinks and making as much noise as possible.

Then, some blazers entered. Navy blue blazers with gold buttons, accompanied by maroon neckties and some stiff-looking, button-down kids. Westside uniforms worn by Westside kids. They were much too clean for kids, much too neat. Their postures were too perfect. Their mothers had never had to tell them to stand up straight when relatives had come to visit, because they were already human rulers.

The enemy. McDonald's got quiet. Very quiet.

One Westside boy stepped forward. "I see you're very busy getting ready for the Great Think-Off Contest," he said, laying on the sarcasm. Every Lewis and Clark kid there wanted to punch him in the nose. Hard.

Danny stepped forward. He matched the Westside kid for sarcasm, pound for pound. "Oh, that simply isn't necessary, Mr. Westside-Kid," he said. "You see, we're already ready."

A Westside girl spoke up. "Pray tell, which of you *geniuses* [she gave the word geniuses its own special dose of sarcasm] will be defending your school's honor in the upcoming practice match?"

The kids from Ms. McCardle's class all pointed to Danny. The Westside kids started to snicker.

"You mean you only have *one kid* for the whole contest?" a Westside kid said. Then he laughed out loud.

"Yeah! That's right!" said Danny. "One kid! *Me!* And I'm gonna beat you all! Right up to your neckties!"

All the Westside kids laughed then and started to leave. As they went, they chanted together in a singsong way, "Losers-losers-losers, losers-losers-losers." They started softly and gradually got louder and louder, "Losers-losers-losers, losers-losers-los—"

"Hey, wait a minute!" said Tommy. "Who are you calling losers? I'm in the contest, too, and I don't like being called a loser, especially when my team, the Lewis and Clark team, is going to win!" His face took on a look of grim determination as he strolled over to Danny.

"*OOOOOOOOH!*" went all the Westside kids.

"I'm *really scared*," said one Westside boy.

Sue Zimmer, a Lewis and Clark girl, pushed her friend Francy Kloss forward. "We can't leave it all up to just Danny and Tommy," Sue whispered. "You're smart. You should be on the team, too."

"I guess I'm in," Francy said, joining Tommy and Danny and laughing a nervous little laugh, "Hee hee, ha-ha."

The Westside girls did a grotesque imitation of her laugh, *"HEE HEE, HA-HA!"* and Francy shot them a kill-look that would have made Ms. McCardle proud.

Martha Coffin, in what was a real burst of energy for her, looked up from her soda and said, "I'm in."

"Eric," Danny whispered, "come on. It'll be fun."

"Ah, ah, sh-sh-sure," Eric stammered.

"SH-SH-SH-SH-SH-SH-SURE . . ." went the Westside kids, and laughed loudly. They finally walked out, saying things like, "S-s-s-see you th-th-there!" and "G-g-g-g-good luck, *L-L-L-L-LOSERS!*"

Silently, the Lewis and Clark kids returned to their fries, their sodas, their conversations. In a few minutes, everything was almost the way it was before the Westside kids came in—almost, but not quite. Something was different. Maybe the fries seemed a little bit crispier, maybe the jokes seemed just a little bit funnier, or maybe, somehow, the Lewis and Clark kids already felt like winners. After all, they had stood up to Westside.

In fact, everyone was so caught up in the good feelings of the moment, that it didn't occur to any of the kids that *feeling* like a winner is quite different from *being* a winner, and that to *be* winners, they might actually have to study. This especially did not occur to Danny, convinced as he was that Homework would take care of everything.

Homework, curled up all alone in a corner of McDonald's, knew otherwise. He's *got* to study, he's just *got* to, Homework thought, as he watched Danny having the time of his life after almost three weeks of being grounded. If he doesn't study, he'll be totally humiliated. Then where will the good feelings come from? It's my job to help him. I can't win it *for* him, but I've got to help him somehow. How? *How?* Ooey kaflooey kachoo, kachoo. Ooey kaflooey machooey mahooey kachoo, kachoo, kachoo, ka . . .

CHAPTER

11

WARP-FREE

Spring vacation. *WARP-FREE!*

McDonald's had been spectacular, but the first moments of coming home and throwing his stuff in his room, the first kicking off of his shoes, the first dinner, and the first chocolate cake of the first vacation from school since Christmas were just as good.

WARP, WARP, WARP, WARP, WARP, WARP-FREE!

After dinner, Danny played H-O-R-S-E in the driveway with his family. All of his practice with the wire hanger hoop in his room paid off. He shot like a real pro.

"Are you sure you've been in your room studying for the last few weeks?" asked Dad. "You look like you've been doing nothing but shooting baskets!"

"Hagh!" Danny spent a few seconds choking, then said, "Uh, uh . . . no . . . no, I . . . I really *was* studying."

Dad laughed and gave Danny a friendly slap on the back. "Of course you were, Dan! You're doin' great!"

After H-O-R-S-E, Danny watched TV and talked on the phone with Eric for about half an hour, planning everything they would do over the vacation.

"What a week we're gonna have!" Danny sang out to Homework, when he came up to his room to get ready for bed. He kicked off his sneakers and plopped down on his bed. "Hey, you really should have come outside with us tonight. It was great!"

Homework was curled up in the middle of the floor. He gave Danny a vacant nod.

"It was great," Danny went on, selling Homework on his plans. "And there will be more! We can watch cartoons every morning. Do you like cartoons? I do. Cartoons are great! Then we can go to the park and meet the guys, there are a couple of movies I want to see, and, oh, yeah, I've got to get my bike fixed up . . ." Danny paused. "What's up?" he asked Homework. "You don't seem excited. I thought you'd be happy to have a little break."

Homework sat up and gave Danny a penetrating glance.

"Come on, what's up?" Danny said. "I've never seen you so serious."

"I don't want to spoil your good time," Homework said, "but I guess something's bothering me. I've been sitting here thinking about it all night long, and I just can't figure it out."

"What?" Danny asked. "Maybe I can help."

"You," said Homework, "I can't figure you out. I go over and over it, and I still can't figure out why you entered the contest, if you want to flunk."

"Easy!" Danny answered. He got down on the floor next to Homework. "You won't believe this, it's so beautiful. Did you hear Mr. Jessup say the contest is *extracurricular?*"

Homework nodded.

Danny continued, "And you heard him say, that means *no credit!*"

"Yes, but I still don't get it."

Danny jumped up. "That means I can ace the contest and still flunk! And—this is the best part—then, when I flunk, everyone will know I'm flunking because I *want to,* and not because I *can't pass.*"

Homework's mouth dropped open. He didn't say anything.

Danny was grinning wildly. "Now do you get it?"

he asked Homework. "Isn't that a brilliant plan?"

The dog took a moment to gather his thoughts, then said, "It's quite an amazing plan, but I have one teeny, tiny, little question. You say you're going to ace the Think-Off Contest."

"Right," said Danny.

"How are you going to do that?" asked Homework. "You haven't opened a book since February."

"Well I sort of thought, you know, you've been so helpful all along, I thought you could sort of help me with the contest."

"Me?" asked Homework.

"Yes," Danny said. "You."

"The very same dog that just this morning you ordered *not* to help you with any more homework?" asked Homework.

"Yes!" Danny exclaimed. He began striding around the room, gesturing with enthusiasm. "Won't it be fantastic!" he went on. "You'll hover invisibly next to me, right on the stage, in front of everybody, and I'll answer question after question! It's the opportunity of a lifetime!"

"But, Danny!" Homework exclaimed. "It wouldn't be *fair*. And besides, it's not my job to sit there and give you all the answers!"

"Of course it is," Danny explained. "That's what you've been doing all along, isn't it?"

"No!" said Homework. "That's not what I was

doing at all! I was trying to get *you* to study! I just wasn't very successful at it, that's all."

Danny had stopped striding around the room. He had stopped gesturing with enthusiasm. He stood very still and looked at Homework with no expression whatsoever on his face.

"Does this mean you won't help me win the contest?" Danny asked.

"I'll help you study," said Homework, "but I can't go there and win it *for* you."

"WHY NOT?" Danny wailed.

"Because it's a *lie!*" Homework exploded. "You know it's a lie! And lying bothers you, doesn't it? It did last night! That's why you felt so bad—you felt bad, didn't you?—when everyone was going crazy over all your *A*'s, and you knew you hadn't earned them."

"The Westsiders are nasty and obnoxious," Danny said. "They deserve to lose."

"Then beat them, fair and square," Homework said.

Danny was silent, his face frozen into a fierce mask.

"You want it both ways," Homework said, "and you can't have it both ways. You want to do nothing, and ace this contest, and have everyone think you're great, but you won't be acing the contest at all, *I* will, and that's a *lie!* I'm sorry, Danny, I can't do it. I'll help you study, but I can't win the contest *for* you."

"I'll study tomorrow," Danny quickly chimed.

"Now," said Homework, "for, say, ten minutes." He leaped up to Danny's desk and pushed a book in Danny's direction.

Danny didn't move.

"Ten minutes isn't so long, Danny," Homework said.

Danny didn't budge. "You talk about *me* being a liar," Danny said, his voice strangely quiet. "Me? What about you?"

"What?" Homework asked.

"You," Danny said. "*You're* the liar. You promised you'd stay and help me 'as long as necessary.' '*As long as necessary,*' those were your very words! And now, *now*, when your help is obviously *necessary*, you break your promise."

"You misunderstood me, Danny," Homework said softly, a pained look on his beagle's face. His eyes had never drooped so low. "I'm sorry, but you misunderstood."

Danny said nothing.

"I'm sorry you think I lied to you," Homework said. "I really was trying to help. If you ever want a study partner, I'll come back. I promise." Homework went over to Danny and licked his hand. "I promise," he repeated. Then he sat down in the middle of the floor. He raised his left paw in the air.

"WHAT ARE YOU DOING?" Danny yelled.

"I'm going," said Homework.

"GOING!?!" Danny shrieked. *"WHERE!?!"*

"Away," said Homework.

"For how long?"

"As long as necessary."

"YOU CAN'T!" screamed Danny. *"WHAT ABOUT THE CONTEST!?!"*

"Study, and I'll come back," said Homework. Then he drew three circles in the air and chanted:

> "Double, double,
> Lots of trouble,
> Now hie me home,
> On the double."

He was gone.

Danny lunged for the spot on the rug where Homework had been sitting just a moment before, but the dog was no longer there. Danny scurried around the room, scouring the corners, grabbing under his bed, tearing through his closet, ripping through his drawers. He threw the bedroom window open and scanned the darkness. "HOMEWORK! HOMEWORK, WHERE ARE YOU?" he called. A dog barked! In a flash, Danny was downstairs and out the front door. He saw nothing.

"HOMEWORK, HOMEWORK!" Danny called, and again the dog barked, but Danny could tell now that it was the loud, low-pitched barking of a very large dog, a Saint Bernard or a Great Dane, maybe, and not Homework's medium-sized *woof*.

Danny sat down on the front steps and caught his breath. Then he raised his left hand, drew three circles in the air, and tried to think up some kind of magical chant that would bring the dog back.

> "Homework, Homework,
>   Hasten hither,"

Danny chanted.
Nothing happened.

> "Homework, Homework,
>   Come hither, come back, come blither, slither,
>   Lither, dither . . ."

That didn't work either. What had Homework said when he left?

> "Double, double,
>   Trouble, trouble,
>   Trouble, trouble,
>   Hasten hither on the double."

There was only quiet. Danny held his head in his hands. All he'd wanted was to save the honor of his school and live *WARP-FREE* at the same time. Now he faced total humiliation.

"Errrrrrrr," Homework cried when he got to Ms. McCardle's house. He sat down on the couch next to her and told her the whole sad story.

Ms. McCardle was very quiet. She took in a deep breath and let it out slowly, then she reached out to Homework and started stroking his back. "You tried to tell me, didn't you?" she asked. "What exactly was it you said just before I sent you to Danny?"

"Arf arf woof woof, arf arf wow wow bow bow, bark arf erf."

"Yes, that's it. You told me the *Plan* was out of date, and I wouldn't listen." Ms. McCardle stopped patting Homework. She looked into the distance, frowning. "Perhaps it is out of date," she said. "Perhaps kids today are smarter, or more stubborn, or simply more terrified than kids were four hundred years ago. Or then again, maybe it's just Danny. Maybe the *Plan* just doesn't work on Danny."

"Arf arf erf erf?" Homework asked.

"I don't know what we're going to do now," said Ms. McCardle, "but I know we can't let Danny down. We must figure out a way to help him. We must think of a new *Plan*. One that works."

Ms. McCardle got down on the floor and started rummaging through the piles of books she had stacked there. She went through pile after pile until she pulled out a large, brown leather-bound book. Its title was, *When All Else Fails,* and its binding looked stiff and smooth, as if it had never been opened.

When Ms. McCardle opened the book the binding made a slight cracking sound and two cups of cocoa and a plate of oatmeal cookies appeared on the coffee table. The book began to read itself to Ms. McCardle and Homework in a comforting, grandmotherly voice: "When all else fails, there is naught to do but try again." The book read itself on through the night.

That spring vacation, Danny didn't watch cartoons, he didn't play ball in the park, he didn't go to the movies, he didn't fix up his bike, and he didn't study.

He looked for Homework. He looked everywhere. He never found him.

When he got back to school after vacation, his class was getting excited about the upcoming practice match. During lunch and in the schoolyard, it was the main topic of conversation.

"We'll ace it," the kids said.

"We'll cream 'em," the kids said.

"They don't stand a chance," the kids said.

"Get 'em, Danny!" the kids said.

They'll *hate* me, Danny thought, then he scanned the far reaches of the playground, praying for a glimpse of a shaggy tan and black dog with a bushy black eyebrow.

Friday. Practice match day. Westside kids filled the seats on one side of the auditorium. Lewis and Clark kids filled the seats on the other side.

The judges entered and sat down.

Mr. Jessup walked over to a podium at the center of the stage and coughed.

The Westside kids entered and sat down at one of two tables set up on the stage. Then they straightened their ties, which were already much too straight and tight for the occasion.

The Westside kids in the audience cheered, "*We want blood! We want blood!*" and stamped their feet— very rowdy behavior for such well-dressed kids.

The seats at the other table, the Lewis and Clark table, remained empty.

"I don't know about you, but I'm just a little bit nervous," Francy Kloss said to her teammates as they huddled together next to the curtains in the wings of the stage.

"Uh-huh," said Martha Coffin.

"Do you think maybe we should have gotten together to study a little bit over vacation?" Francy asked.

No one answered.

"Danny should be here any minute," Eric said, scanning the backstage area for a glimpse of his friend.

"Why isn't he here?" Tommy asked.

"He went to the bathroom," said Francy. "Remember, he left math to go to the bathroom."

"That was half an hour ago," said Martha.

Tommy laughed a sarcastic laugh. "That's great," he said, "just great. He gets us into this thing, and then he doesn't even show up!"

"He'll be here," Eric said. "What's your problem?"

Mr. Jessup was still standing at the podium in the center of the stage. He coughed. Then he held his hand like a visor over his eyes to help him see into the darkness of the backstage area.

"I guess the children . . ." (the whole audience groaned) "have encountered a slight delay," he said into the microphone. "Um, er, excuse me—uh, just a moment." He walked backstage to the Lewis and Clark kids. A few seconds later, he came back, quite alone.

In the wings, Tommy spoke again. "Danny's a

loser, and he always will be. I'm not waiting for him one more second." He strolled onstage, waving to the audience.

"Do you think we should go out?" Francy asked Martha and Eric.

"You girls go ahead," Eric said to Francy and Martha. "I'll wait for Danny."

Francy and Martha walked onto the stage.

Mr. Jessup watched the kids sit down. He waited a second, then he went over to them.

"Is that it?" he whispered to the Lewis and Clark kids.

Francy nodded.

Mr. Jessup sighed. He walked back to the podium and spoke into the microphone. "Oh, well. Let the practice match begin."

The match was over fairly quickly. Lewis and Clark got slaughtered. Eric waited patiently for Danny backstage, but by the end of the match, Danny still had not returned from the bathroom.

A few blocks away, Danny lay on his bed and threw a crumpled paper ball across his bedroom.

Throw, miss.

Then he threw another. And another.

Throw, miss. Throw, miss. Throw . . .

YOU CAN'T CATCH ME, 'CUZ I'M WARP-FREE!

"O Captain! My Captain!"

*M*onday morning after the practice match, Ms. McCardle was just about to start the English lesson when Danny shuffled in. He was an hour late for school. Homework, who was sitting next to Ms. McCardle's desk, visible to her but invisible to everyone else, watched Danny walk slowly to his seat.

Not one of the kids laughed, not even Tommy Lewis. No one made a sound. Danny had gotten them all involved, then he had let them down. The kids glared at Danny, the coward.

"Take your seat, Danny," Ms. McCardle said gently, ignoring Danny's lateness. "Everybody, please take out your English books."

Danny shuffled over to Ms. McCardle at her desk.

"I quit," he muttered. Then he shuffled to his seat.

The room was so quiet, it was as if all sound had been sucked out of it by a huge sound vacuum cleaner.

"May I see you in the hall for a moment please, Danny?" Ms. McCardle asked.

She held the classroom door open, and Danny shuffled out. Homework shuffled invisibly after him.

"I'm sorry," Danny said in the hall, so quietly that Ms. McCardle could barely hear him. "I know I let everyone down." He stared at the tiny brown and gold flecks in the tiles of the floor. If he scrunched his eyes into little slits, the flecks looked like tiny brown bugs, dancing and wearing fancy gold costumes.

"That's right, you did let everyone down," said Ms. McCardle. "It wasn't a very nice thing to do. You surprised me, Danny. I didn't think you were that sort of a person. What's it going to be now? You know none of the kids would have signed up for the contest if you hadn't challenged those Westsiders."

Danny looked up at her in surprise.

Homework, hovering invisibly next to Ms. McCardle, watched Danny closely.

"Oh, yes," Ms. McCardle continued. "I heard all about it. I was told those Westside kids were extremely nasty and obnoxious, and you stood right up to them."

"They *were* obnoxious," Danny said. "They were really awful."

"Were they right?" Ms. McCardle asked. "Are we losers? Do we give up without even trying?"

Danny said nothing.

"It's my fault, too," said Ms. McCardle. "I didn't help you kids get organized, I didn't help you study, and I really should have. Now, I'm prepared to give the Think-Off Team a half hour of in-class study time a day, and I have a workbook of practice questions, *A Super Fifth Grader's Super Workbook,* which I think will be very helpful. If you kids want me to, I'll meet with you all after school a couple of times a week to help you study. You know, Danny, the final match is still six weeks away. If you study, you stand a good chance."

Danny said nothing.

"I'll give you a moment to think it over," said Ms. McCardle, and went back into the classroom. Homework floated to the ground and invisibly followed her.

Ms. McCardle sat down at her desk, leaned over, and opened the bottom right-hand drawer. Homework knew she was doing this so she could talk to him without the kids overhearing her.

"Roof roof WOOF!?!" he asked.

"It's the new *Plan*," Ms. McCardle whispered. "We *have* to motivate him."

"Arf *woof?*" Homework asked.

"What's wrong with *guilt?*" Ms. McCardle whispered.

"*ARF!*" Homework sputtered, and threw up his paws.

"It was in the book, *When All Else Fails*, remember, right at the beginning of chapter three?" Ms. McCardle whispered. "I admit, it seems unorthodox, but if it gets him going, I say it's justified. You notice I threw in a little revenge, too? That was in chapter four."

Meanwhile, Danny was still out in the hall, thinking over what Ms. McCardle had said. He had never really had a problem with *studying*, his problem was with *WARPING*, with having no choice.

If I study, maybe I will do fine, Danny thought. Maybe I do owe it to my friends. I did get them into this mess. And after all, those Westsiders really do deserve to lose.

Danny opened the door to the classroom. All activity in the room stopped as Danny entered.

Danny took a deep breath and nodded at Ms. McCardle.

Invisibly, Homework smiled at Ms. McCardle, and visibly, Ms. McCardle smiled at Danny. "Good for you," she said. Then she addressed her class.

"We have a Think-Off Team," she said. "The team members are really putting themselves on the line for our school, and I think it's important that we support them in their efforts. With that end in mind, I will allow the members of the team a half hour of in-class study time a day. Your time for today will start now."

Danny walked over to his desk and pushed it to the back of the room. His teammates did not move.

"You know," said Ms. McCardle, "one person does not make a team." She looked around the room and focused on Eric, then Francy, then Martha, then Tommy. "I thought there were more of you on this team," she said. "Those of you who signed up have made a commitment. Fifth graders know how to follow through on their commitments, don't they?"

"*Uhhhhg,*" the teammates moaned softly, then, "*Ahhhhrg.*" Nevertheless, *BANG* went the desks, *SCRAPE* went the desks. *CLUNK* went Eric and Danny, *BONK* went Francy, Martha, and Tommy, and *PLOP* went the teammates into their chairs, at their desks, at the back of the room.

Homework walked invisibly over to them.

"I'll give you a half hour of class time a day, and I can help you after school on Tuesdays and Thursdays. Maybe you can take turns going to each other's houses on the other days to study," Ms.

McCardle added. "I know if you all help each other you'll enjoy your studying more, and get more out of it. Get to work now. I'd like the rest of the class to take out their English anthologies and open them to page 238, where we'll continue with our analysis of Walt Whitman's poem, "O Captain! My Captain!"

"*SIGH,*" went the teammates. There they were. The team. They had six weeks left until the Great Think-Off Contest.

The teammates looked at each other. They looked at Ms. McCardle. No one would make the first move. There they sat. And sat. And sat.

Why doesn't he do something? Homework thought.

Danny sighed. "This is silly," he said. "We're not getting anything done."

"Well, now that you actually decided to show up, Mr. No-Show, we're very sorry that we're not living up to your high standards," said Tommy Lewis.

"Look. OK, look," Danny said to his teammates. "I'm sorry about Friday." No one said anything. "I'm really sorry I let you down." They all just looked at him.

"Did you get sick or something, Danny?" Francy asked.

"Naw, naw," Danny answered. What could he say? Explaining about Homework was out of the question. He'd tried that once before, with embarrassing results. "I guess I got a little freaked out," Danny said to the group. "You know, it's one thing to be up in front of the class, but there were so many people in that auditorium, and well . . ."

"I understand," said Eric. "There *were* a lot of people there. I find large crowds upsetting sometimes, too."

"I notice *you* never quite made it onstage either," said Tommy.

"I was waiting for Danny!" Eric snapped.

Tommy and Eric glared at each other, and still no one studied.

Why doesn't he do something? Homework thought, as he invisibly sat in on the *un*study session.

"Well, you know what?" Danny asked. "My house is good on Wednesdays. After school on Wednesdays, we could go to my house."

"Mine is better because my mom makes cookies on Tuesday nights," said Eric.

"What about my house?" whined Tommy.

"Your little brother always smells bad," Eric explained.

"He does not!" argued Tommy.

"He does so," Eric added. "After all, I mean, the kid wears diapers. And you and I both know what goes into *DIAPERS*."

"We don't have a baby at my house," said Martha.

"We use air freshener at my house," said Francy. "My house always smells like sweet balsa wood."

"My house smells better!" Tommy yelled.

"I don't believe this," said Danny.

"Mine smells great!" Eric screamed.

"*MINE!*" cried Tommy.

"*NO MINE!*" shrieked Martha.

"*NO MINE!*" screeched Francy.

"Who cares what anybody's house *SMELLS LIKE!?!*" bellowed Danny.

"*QUIET!*" yelled Ms. McCardle.

She walked over to where they were all sitting at the back of the room. She nodded at Homework, then spoke to the group. "Having trouble getting organized?" she asked cheerfully.

The team was quiet.

"Hmm. I thought so," Ms. McCardle said.

"Thought what?" Tommy asked. "No one said anything."

Sometimes even Ms. McCardle didn't know what to do with Tommy. "Maybe you need a captain," she said, speaking to the group. Each kid nodded politely and smiled at her, hoping that would get her to leave. It almost worked. She moved away from their desks. But she was only thinking. She came back. "I think Danny would make a very good captain. Will you be captain, Danny?"

Danny nodded.

"Does everyone agree to this?" Ms. McCardle asked the team.

Everyone nodded and smiled, and Ms. McCardle finally left.

"Herr, herr, herr." Homework laughed silently to himself.

Ms. McCardle chuckled softly to herself at the front of the room.

"OK," Danny said. "Study schedule. Everyone take this down."

Out came paper and pencils.

"First week," Danny went on, "starting tonight, we'll have math at Martha's house. Tomorrow, Tuesday—social studies here with Ms. McCardle then after, at my house. Wednesday—science at Eric's, and Thursday—English here and at Tommy's. Friday we'll meet at Francy's and start over on our subjects with math. Saturday we'll be at Martha's again, and so on. OK?"

Francy, Martha, and Eric nodded silently.

"Bu—bu—but . . ." Tommy whispered, then stopped when he got kill-looks from each of his teammates.

"OK, now open your math books," Danny whispered. "What do we think of Westside? Remember McDonalds!?!"

"Let's get 'em!" Tommy said, and the five teammates opened their math books.

CHAPTER

13

Homework Dogs

The teammates stuck to their study schedule and studied hard.

Danny studied hard, but he was rusty. His teammates had to help him.

One day after school the team was at Francy's house.

"What is the Gettysburg Address?" Martha read from the workbook Ms. McCardle had loaned them.

"The Gettysburg Address," Danny said thoughtfully. "That's where George Washington lived, isn't it?" Danny asked. "Right? It was his address."

Danny's teammates stared at him.

"Wasn't he getting straight A's for awhile," Tommy asked no one in particular.

"The Gettysburg Address is a speech, Danny," said Martha. "It's a famous speech."

"OK," said Danny. "A speech. Ohhhh! Easy—it's a speech George Washington gave."

"*Get with it!*" Tommy bellowed.

Homework hovered invisibly at just the right height and gave Tommy a little nudge in the seat of his pants.

"*Knock it off!*" Tommy yelled.

"I didn't *do* anything!" Danny yelled back.

Danny never told Mom and Dad about the practice match, and how he hadn't shown up, but he did tell them he was captain of the Think-Off team.

"Look how you've turned yourself around!" Mom said, and gave him a hug.

"That's great, Danny," Dad said. "Just great!"

Then Danny's family helped him study, everyone except Evie and Judy. Evie and Judy wanted to help Danny, but Evie was only four and knew very little, and Judy was only plastic and knew even less.

So every night, Danny, Mom, Dad, and Grandma (whenever she was over) took turns playing with Evie and Judy, helping with the after-dinner cleanup, and asking questions out of Ms. McCardle's workbook. The grown-ups loved it. Grandma had so much fun that she stayed for dinner more and more often.

"What kind of houses did the Iroquois Indians live in?" Mom read from the workbook one night, while Dad loaded the dishwasher.

"I know that one!" Dad yelled, so excited he almost dropped a cup. "The Iroquois lived in longhouses. Not tepees, Danny, but longhouses."

"It was my turn, Dad," Danny said, as he wrapped up the leftover hamburgers.

"It was Danny's turn, Alan," said Grandma while she zoomed a toy car to Evie and Judy.

"Sorry," said Dad. "Danny, you take the next one."

"What country first introduced horses to the New World?" Mom read.

"Uh, France," said Danny.

"No way, *José*," said Mom, giving Danny an encouraging look.

"Uh, England," said Danny.

"No way, *JOSÉ!*" Mom said, louder this time.

Danny looked at her blankly.

"I didn't know you spoke *Spanish*, honey," Dad said. "Isn't that the language they speak in the country of . . ."

"I know! It's SPAIN!" Danny yelled. "The answer is *SPAIN!*"

"Good, Danny," Mom, Dad, and Grandma said together, trying not to look worried.

Homework hovered invisibly near the table and checked out the oatmeal cookies everyone was having for dessert.

Before Danny went up to bed, he could have sworn he saw paw prints on the table.

A few days later, at the after school session, Ms. McCardle held the practice test book.

"I'd like to give Danny a chance to answer this one first," said Ms. McCardle. "The rest of you, do the problem, but give Danny a chance to answer first. Danny, how much is twenty-nine times eight point nine?"

Danny jotted down the problem and worked out the answer.

"Two hundred and fifty-eight point one," said Danny.

"Right," said Ms. McCardle.

"Right," said the kids.

"Right," said Danny.

Danny could have sworn he felt someone panting into his left ear, but when he turned to look, there was no one there. However, Danny was almost certain he could detect the slightly sour odor of dog breath in the air.

*   *   *

At bedtime that night, Danny brought a box of oatmeal cookies up to his room, placed it on his desk
where he could see it easily from his bed, then pretended to go to sleep. It wasn't long before the box
started to move, just a little bit.

"All right, Homework, come on out," said Danny.

The box stopped moving.

"Too late," said Danny. "I know you're here."

Homework appeared. "I just wanted to see how
you were doing," the dog said.

"What do you think?" Danny asked.

"Looks like you're doing great!"

There was a moment of silence.

"I'm sorry I called you a liar," Danny said. "I
know you were just trying to help me."

"Thanks," said Homework.

"Are you going to say sorry for calling *me* a liar?"
Danny asked.

"No," said Homework. "You were. Want to
study?"

"OK," said Danny.

"What was the starting point of the Oregon
Trail?" Homework asked.

Danny laughed. "Hey, wasn't that the thing . . .
that first night you came, wasn't that the thing you
pretended not to know?" Danny asked.

Homework nodded.

"Independence, Missouri," said Danny.

The days went by. Danny studied at school during in-class study time, he studied after school with the team, he studied after dinner with his family, and he met Homework in his room every night at bedtime and studied for about half an hour then. It paid off. Danny improved steadily.

The whole team improved steadily. They found that they all had different strengths. Francy was great at math. Martha was great at English. Tommy was great at social studies, especially the parts about wars. Eric was incredibly fast and great at everything, and Danny found out he liked science more than he'd realized before. After awhile they went nuts from studying all the time, so they stopped meeting on the weekends. But they were doing fine, so it was OK to take a break.

As the Great Think-Off Contest drew closer, there were decisions to be made, details to be attended to.

"We need a team name," Danny said one day at practice.

"How about *Predators?*" Tommy asked.

"How about *The Continental Congressmen*," Eric suggested.

"Not all of us are men," Martha said.

"How about *Hearts and Rainbows*," suggested Francy.

"Not all of us are girls," said Tommy.

"How about the *Homework Dogs?*" Danny asked the team.

Everyone except Danny hated that one, and yet after that, no one referred to the team as anything else. Somehow, it fit.

One day they each brought a T-shirt from home down to Francy's basement. Danny also brought a sketch of Homework, all ready for everyone to copy onto their T-shirts with special fabric paints Francy had.

"Great uniforms!" Danny said, and they all agreed.

"Now we need a team slogan," Danny said. "I have the perfect one—Ooey kaflooey kachoo, ka-choo."

The team members said nothing.

"Try saying it," Danny said. "It's fun to say. And it really does keep bad stuff from happening."

"Ooey kaflooey kachoo, kachoo," the teammates said together.

"It's ridiculous!" said Francy.

"Yeah," said Martha. "That's why it's good."

Another day, over at Danny's house, Danny brought up the question of transportation to the contest.

Tommy freaked out. "Don't you remember?" he shrieked.

"What, Tommy, what do you remember?" Danny asked.

"The bus! The bus! It broke down one year! The team never even got to the contest!" Tommy wailed.

Martha tried to calm him down. "Just because it happened once doesn't mean it's going to—"

"*NO!!! NO!!!*" Tommy had screeched. "It'll break down with us on it!!! And we've worked so hard!!!" He was hysterical. When Danny's mom came home from work, Tommy was standing on the dining room table screaming, "*Don't make me! I CAN'T RIDE THE BUS! YOU CAN'T MAKE ME!!!*"

"I'll take everyone in the van," Mom said, when she understood what the problem was.

Danny kept studying with Homework every night.

A few nights before the contest, the dog seemed strangely serious.

"What's up?" Danny asked. "You're too serious."

"I can't come with you to the contest," Homework said.

"Oh," Danny said. "Why not? You know, I don't expect you to answer any questions for me. You could just hang out, you know, and hover next to me."

"It would be nice," said Homework. "But I can't.

I don't trust myself. You may not know this about me, never having seen me in any sort of a contest, but I'm a very competitive dog. If I was there, next to you, I might not be able to control myself. I might cheat. Not that you would need me to cheat, of course. It's strictly my problem."

"What if you tried really hard not to help me?" Danny asked.

"It's not worth the risk," said Homework.

Danny didn't say anything. He patted Homework gently.

"You'll do great," the dog said quietly. "I know it."

"Yeah?" said Danny, "and what if I don't?"

"Do the best you can," said Homework. "It's great just to do the best you can."

Danny had borrowed Dad's stopwatch for the last couple of practice days, so the team could figure out exactly how long it took them to answer a question. They kept track of the times for the whole practice session, then when it was over, they averaged them out.

The day before the contest, the Lewis and Clark Think-Off Team, the Homework Dogs, as they called themselves, were down to an average response time of six seconds.

"Are we *fast?*" Danny asked his teammates.

"Yes!" they answered.

"Are we gonna *win?*" Danny asked.

"*Yes!*" shouted his team.

"Are we *UNBEATABLE?*" Danny asked.

"*YES!!!*" shouted the team.

The only problem was, that in another house, all the way across town, with their average response time down to an all-time low of five seconds, the Westside team felt exactly the same way.

CHAPTER

14

Show Biz

*F*riday night, the night before the Great Think-Off Contest, Danny left nothing to chance. He borrowed both Grandma's and his parents' alarm clocks and he placed them, along with his own, right by his bed. He set them to go off at five-minute intervals, starting at 7:00 A.M. It turned out he didn't need any of them. He woke up at 6:51 A.M. Saturday morning, without any help, in the middle of a dream about the contest. He had dreamed that he was on the stage of the auditorium with his teammates, and Homework was at the microphone, asking questions. Every time Danny got one right, Homework leaped up to the ceiling, hovered there for a minute, and laughed his beagle's head off, "Herr, herr, herr!"

Wide awake, Danny switched off the alarms, got out of bed, and walked slowly to his desk chair, where he had carefully laid out all his clothes for the contest the night before. He put on his lucky sweatpants, the ones with the Lakers patch, in which he had made more penalty shots than in any other pair. He pulled on his favorite socks and his new black high tops. Then he put on his red Homework Dog T-shirt.

Now Danny looked down and patted the picture of Homework on his chest. "This is it, Homework, the big day," Danny said softly to the picture. "The day we get back at Westside. The day I make sure that when I flunk at the end of the year everyone knows I'm really smart. Unless, of course, I blow the whole contest. Then everyone will think I can't do anything. Ooey kaflooey kachoo, kachoo."

All over the city that Saturday morning, fifth graders were getting up early, saying magic words, rubbing rabbits' feet, throwing up, performing exotic toothbrushing rituals, and doing weird dances around the breakfast table, all to ready their brains for academic warfare.

Eric Bedemeyer woke up early that morning and felt a little tense, so he took out his stamp collection. "Ooey kaflooey kachoo, kachoo," he said.

Martha woke up early, too. She sat in bed for a

long time looking at her toes. "Ooey kaflooey ka-choo, kachoo," she whispered.

Francy got up and wrote the speech she planned on giving when her team won. Ooey kaflooey ka-choo, kachoo, was her closing line. Tommy woke up, happy and chipper as usual. We worked so hard, he thought. What if they win? What if we blow it? What if we . . . he ran to the bathroom to throw up. "Ooey kaflooey kachoo, kachoo," he said into the toilet bowl.

Only the Westside team seemed completely un-affected by what lay ahead. By 8:25 A.M., each team member was washed, necktied, breakfasted, and briefcased to perfection. By 8:30 A.M., each kid was waiting like a shiny young executive statuette at his or her front door for the limo and chauffeur they had hired for the occasion.

At 8:25 A.M. at Ms. McCardle's house, an argu-ment was taking place.

"*Arf woof! Bark roof GRRRRRRR!*" Homework raged.

"Really, Homework," said Ms. McCardle, "I don't think it's anything to growl over."

"*GRRRRRRRRRRRRRRRR!!!*"

"All right, fine. If you really feel that strongly about it you may come along. I can understand your wanting to see Danny at the contest. But you worry me. I know your competitive nature. Under no circumstances may you let Danny know you are there, and you must promise me you won't help him with any answers. Do you promise?"

Homework drew a cross on his chest with his right paw. Then he raised his paw in the air. "Woof," he promised.

Meanwhile, at 8:30 A.M. at Danny's house, the Homework Dogs waited for Danny's mom to start up the family van.

"Good luck, Danny," Dad said, and hugged his son. "I'll see you later, when I bring Evie."

"I love you, Danny," Evie said, and hugged her brother. Then, holding her Judy doll up to his face, and making her voice even higher and squeakier than it already was, she said, "I love you, too, Danny." Danny stared at the doll. "Kiss her," Evie commanded in her regular voice, "or she'll think you don't love her." The doll's glow-in-the-dark fluorescent hair was a bright, blinding pink.

Danny saw Mom watching him. If she got mad, she might not drive them to the contest, and then they'd be late. Quick, *yuck*, it was over.

Tommy was laughing so hard he was crying. It was the best he'd felt all day.

"Ooh, isn't that cute?" Francy gushed.

"OK, show's over," said Danny. "Let's get outta here."

Mom and the five members of the Lewis and Clark

Homework Dog team climbed into the van. A quick turn of the key in the ignition, and they were off.

When the team walked through the stage door of the auditorium, they were greeted by a scene that looked like it belonged more in Hollywood than in a medium-sized midwestern town. Television crews were everywhere, handling all kinds of technical-looking stuff, and talking to each other on walkie-talkies. Cameras were rolling, reporters were reporting, and flashbulbs were flashing, as photographers snapped shots of the arriving teams. One flashbulb went off a little too close to Tommy, and he had to run to the bathroom to throw up again.

"We're in show biz!" Danny said, grinning for the photographers.

"I'm famous!" whispered Francy excitedly, then she laughed her nervous little laugh. "I didn't know there would be so much . . . so much . . . well, *ME-DIA!!!*" Then she shook her perm and struck a glamorous pose.

Teams from all over the city were arranged in clumps everywhere—on the stage, in the wings, in the orchestra, and in the balcony. Each team seemed to be wearing its own special outfit or uniform. One team was dressed in black and green Mohawk hairdos, another team had on extra-baggy balloon tops and tight pants, while another had tight tops and balloon bottoms. One team was outfitted so that when the teammates stood next to each other, they formed an American flag. There was even a team that had fully outfitted each teammate in a clown suit, complete with whiteface, rainbow wig, big floppy shoes, and a red ball nose, their theory being that looking silly would help them relax. They all huddled together and bit their nails.

And, of course, there were the Westside kids, straightening their ties, brushing off their blazers, and posing for the photographers.

"The T-shirts look pretty good, don't you think?" Danny asked the team.

"Yeah," they all said, halfheartedly.

"You don't think we're slightly underdressed?" Francy asked.

"Nah," said Danny. "T-shirts are classic."

Suddenly, the auditorium was blasted by the unmistakable sound of someone blowing into a microphone. *"WHHHH! WHHHH! WHHHH!"* The mayor's wife, Mrs. Curtizon, who was going to emcee the contest, was standing at the microphone at the podium in the center of the stage. "I don't think it's on," she said, tapping the microphone several times. This made a sound loud enough to knock everyone to Chicago and back. *"TAP, TAP, TAP, TAP, TAP!"* Next came a terrible squeak that shattered everyone's eardrums until a technician finally turned the right knob and stopped it.

"Excuse me, everybody, excuse me, please," Mrs. Curtizon said into the microphone. "Will all teams, with the exceptions of the teams from Eastern Hills Elementary and Ferdinand Magellan Elementary, please take their assigned seats in the auditorium? Eastern Hills and Ferdinand Magellan, please report to the backstage area, as you'll be competing in the first round. Please be seated, kids, we have to start admitting the audience. Thank you."

All the teams, except for Eastern Hills and Ferdinand Magellan, wandered to seats reserved for them in the front ten rows of the middle section of the auditorium. Then the ushers opened the doors to the lobby and floods of people surged through the doors. Within minutes, the auditorium seemed fuller than it could ever get, and still the people kept coming. The place got noisier by the second. There were babies screaming, parents and grandparents screaming at them to stop, and teenagers so busy looking cool, they were audibly silent. Everyone had come to share in the excitement of the day.

"Please take seats, everybody," Mrs. Curtizon said into the microphone. "We'd like to get started in a few minutes. And will the Eastern Hills team please report to the backstage area immediately? Thank you."

If anything, the crowd in the auditorium just got crazier, and the crazier they got, the quieter the Dogs became. Francy examined her ring with the little hearts on it that her cousin from New York had sent her for Christmas. Tommy drank some warm Coke to try and settle his stomach. Danny kept patting the picture of Homework on his shirt. Martha read her program, over, and over, and over, and over, and Eric started looking very weird. His eyes got sort of blank and vacant, and his mouth was just kind of hanging there, loose and open.

"Oh my goodness!" Martha exclaimed, staring at her program.

"What?" asked Danny and Francy together.

"Look," Martha said ominously, pointing.

"Oh, wow," Danny said in disbelief. "We're second."

"What?" Eric asked in a daze.

"We're supposed to go second," Danny said quietly.

Eric started breathing faster and faster.

"Get him!" Francy said to Danny, and Danny was just able to catch Eric when he passed out. Danny's mom ran to get some water. Mrs. Curtizon saw Eric from the stage and rushed to help.

"I'm a nurse," she said, and started looking him over. "He's probably just nervous."

"No wonder he finked out of the practice match!

Nervous? Just look at him!" Tommy shouted. He was hysterical. He had to sip his Coke quietly for a moment to recover, so that he wouldn't have to make another emergency visit to the bathroom.

Danny's mom came back with the water. Tommy grabbed the cup from her and poured the water all over Eric.

"*I'm sorry!*" Tommy screamed. "I guess I shouldn't have done that. I just thought, well, you know, they do that in the movies, and . . ."

"No thanks, Mom, no more bacon," Eric mumbled, coming to.

"I'm not your mom," Danny said. "And I don't have any bacon."

Eric looked up into Danny's face. "Nothing personal, Danny, but why are you hugging me?"

"You passed out," Danny answered, as he helped Eric sit up.

"Do you feel all right now?" Mrs. Curtizon asked. Eric nodded, and Mrs. Curtizon gave him a quick once over right there in the auditorium in front of everybody. She asked him nurse-questions, like how many fingers was she holding up and did he feel dizzy—stuff like that.

When it was clear that Eric really was all right, Mrs. Curtizon went back to her emcee duties.

"I was afraid you weren't gonna make it," Danny said.

"I'm fine," said Eric, "really fine." Then he made the horrible mistake of looking around the auditorium at the other teams, and as soon as he did, he started to look weird again. His eyes went blank and his breath came faster and faster.

"Quick!" said Danny. "Put your head down." Eric did as he was told.

"Thank you very much," Eric said politely.

"No problem," Danny replied.

Mrs. Curtizon's voice blasted over the loudspeakers. "You must find seats, everybody! We'd like to begin in five minutes. Please go to your designated seating area. There are still a lot of seats left over here," she said, pointing to the left side of the auditorium.

The crowd finally calmed down. They were ready to see what they had come to see. Only a few stragglers remained standing, and they would soon be seated.

"We'll start as soon as the Eastern Hills team reports to the stage," Mrs. Curtizon went on. "Eastern Hills, we're waiting for you!"

The Dogs sat in silence. Not a bark, not a whimper did they make. All around them, the other teams were getting ready. The American flag team was studying a diagram of the digestive system. The balloon top, tight pants team and the tight top, balloon bottom team, were having an impromptu spelling bee. The team with the black and green

Mohawks was having a heated discussion of post–World War II economic growth in Communist bloc countries, and a girl from the clown team was reading aloud to her fellow Bozos from a joke book.

Meanwhile, it was clear that Eric could not budge from his bent over position without passing out.

As captain, Danny felt he had to do something, but he had no idea what. How could he get Eric to stay conscious, when one look at the crowd sent him into never-never land? "We worked so hard," Danny said. "We can't give up now. Eric, we need you." Danny hung his head down next to Eric's so that he could talk directly to him. "We're all smart, but when you're not busy fainting, you're faster than any of us. And, unfortunately, against those Westside kids, we need speed."

"Excuse me, excuse me," Mrs. Curtizon's voice came over the speakers. "I have to announce a slight change in the program. We've just learned that the bus carrying the team from Eastern Hills Elementary has broken down . . ."

"See, I *told* you so," Tommy whispered to his teammates. "At least we're *here*."

"And," Mrs. Curtizon continued, "we'd like the Lewis and Clark Homework Dogs to report to the stage immediately. They will be taking Eastern Hills' place in the first round of the day against Ferdinand Magellan Elementary."

"That's it," said Francy.

"We're done for," muttered Tommy.

"Everybody think!" Danny said. "There's got to be something we can do to help Eric!"

They all thought harder than they'd ever thought before in their lives, but it was Martha who finally bent over in her seat and hung her head down next to Eric's to speak to him. "Try putting your hands up next to your eyes," she said. "Use your hands sort of like they use blinders on a horse." She demonstrated from her bent over position so that Eric would know what in the world she was talking about.

Eric didn't do anything.

"I see what she's getting at," Danny said. "Try it." Eric did nothing. "Try it already!" Danny yelled. "We're all counting on you! It can't *hurt*!"

"I'm not a horse!" Eric grumbled. Nevertheless, he made his hands into blinders and held them up next to his eyes, just as Martha had done.

"And stay that way!" Tommy commanded.

"Lewis and Clark! We're waiting for you!" Mrs. Curtizon called into the microphone. "Don't tell me their bus broke down too."

"No, we're here!" Danny yelled from his seat. "We'll be there in just a minute. Just give us a minute, please!"

"Oh," said Mrs. Curtizon, scanning the audience to locate the boy speaking to her. Danny waved to her. "Aren't you the captain of the team . . . um . . .

the boy who fainted—wasn't he on your team?" Mrs. Curtizon said when she found Danny.

Some members of the audience giggled.

"Yes," Danny answered.

"How's he doing?" Mrs. Curtizon asked.

"Just fine," Danny answered. "We'll be right there."

More of the audience giggled.

"Ready when you are," said Mrs. Curtizon.

"Hold this!" Francy directed, handing Eric her ring with the little hearts on it that her cousin had given her for Christmas. "I was going to wear it for luck, but I think you need it more."

"That's very nice, Francy," said Danny. "But we've got to hurry now."

Francy shoved the ring down on Eric's left pinky.

"Oh, come on," Eric whined. "How ridiculous do you want me to look?"

"*Wear it!*" Francy barked. "It's lucky, I told you!"

"Now just imagine," Martha said patiently. "Imagine we're at my house, and Danny's just turned off the cartoons, and taken Francy's magazine away, and gotten me to come down from my room, and you're showing us how to divide decimals. There's no one here but Francy, and Tommy, and Danny, and you, and me; no judges, no other teams, no audience; just us."

"This isn't gonna work," Tommy whined.

"Oh Tommy, shut up," Eric said, his head still three inches from the floor, his hands held like blinders next to his eyes. "It *is* working."

"I can see that," Tommy said sarcastically. "You look just terrific. Sort of like an upside-down horse."

"Excuse me, Lewis and Clark," said Mrs. Curtizon over the microphone. "Are you almost ready?"

"Here we come!" yelled Danny.

The same members of the audience that had giggled before, giggled again, louder.

"We've got to go now," Danny said to Eric. "I know you can do it."

"Just imagine!" said Martha.

"Keep imagining!" said Francy.

"Pathetic," muttered Tommy.

"Keep imagining, and slowly try to sit up," coached Martha.

Eric tried. About halfway up, he got dizzy, and grabbed onto the arms of his chair with his hand-blinders. He accidentally caught a glimpse of the crowd and started breathing fast again. Quick as she could, Francy reached over and put her hands up to Eric's eyes.

"Put your blinders back on," she whispered.

Eric did as he was told. "I think you guys are going to have to steer me," he said.

"*WHAT?*" shrieked Tommy.

"Can't you see I can't use my hands?" Eric bellowed. "And I'm still a little dizzy."

Danny took one of Eric's elbows. Martha took the other. That way they could hold onto Eric and he could still hold his hands up to his eyes. They managed to ease him up to a sitting position, and once he got that far, Eric found that if he kept his blinders up, his head a little bent down, and kept imagining like crazy, he could stay conscious. Whether he could answer contest questions or not remained to be seen.

Slowly, the team started for the stage. Danny and Martha steered Eric, Tommy walked next to Danny, clutching his upset stomach with one hand and holding a can of warm Coke in the other, and Francy, not to be left out, clung to Martha. Side by side, the Homework Dogs started up the broad stairs that led to the stage.

"Ooey kaflooey kachoo, kachoo," Danny whispered over and over, and one by one, his teammates joined in the whispered chant.

The higher the Homework Dogs got, the more people in the audience could see them, and the more people could see them, the more people laughed. By the time they got to their table, the entire audience was hysterical.

"Now that's what I call teamwork!" said Mrs.

Curtizon into the microphone, and most of the audience applauded.

In fact, the only people not applauding were the members of the Westside team. "Look at them. What a bunch of losers," their captain whispered to his teammates. "I don't know why they even bothered to come."

The Dogs seated themselves at a long table, stage left, and waited.

CHAPTER

15

Think-Off

"**W**e'll begin," Mrs. Curtizon said into the microphone. "When did Columbus discover America?"

Danny heard the question, and his hand went up. It was easy. He didn't even have to think about it. One second, his right hand was resting on the table, the next second, it was in the air, almost as if it had decided on its own to be there.

Danny's hand was up, but even with one hand shielding both eyes, Eric got his free hand up faster.

"Yes, Eric," said Mrs. Curtizon.

"1492," Eric answered.

The history judge nodded from the judges' table. Danny was surprised to see that the social studies judge was Ms. McCardle.

The audience applauded.

"Good job," Danny whispered to his friend.

"I think I'm OK now," Eric whispered back.

"Who was the first explorer to sail completely around the world?" Mrs. Curtizon asked.

A couple of hands went up, but Francy was the fastest.

"Francy?" said Mrs. Curtizon.

"Ferdinand Magellan," Francy answered, and flashed the audience a big smile. Ms. McCardle nodded, the audience applauded, and the kids from Ferdinand Magellan Elementary looked like they wished they could disappear.

"Good job," Danny whispered to Francy.

"What is chlorophyll?" Mrs. Curtizon asked.

Again Danny's hand went up. But a Ferdinand Magellan kid was faster.

"Steven," said Mrs. Curtizon.

"Chlorophyll is the stuff . . . wait . . ." Steven paused. "OK, OK," he went on, "it's the stuff . . . yeah . . . it's the stuff you, uh, put on a handkerchief and you put in the jar with the bugs so you don't squoosh them when you kill them, and then you can dissect them and learn all about them."

"I'm sorry, Steven," said Mrs. Curtizon, "that is incorrect. Would anyone from the Lewis and Clark team care to answer now?"

Danny's hand was in the air. To Danny, it seemed

like nothing in the world had ever moved faster. Nothing human anyway.

"Danny?" said Mrs. Curtizon.

"Chlorophyll is the green coloring matter of leaves and plants, essential to the production of carbohydrates by photosynthesis," Danny answered.

The science judge nodded.

"That is correct," said Mrs. Curtizon.

The audience applauded.

Invisibly, Homework leaped up to the ceiling, floated down, and slobbered Ms. McCardle's left ear. Danny happened to notice her wriggling strangely. Then she took out a handkerchief and wiped her ear.

The match continued. Eric stayed conscious, and did brilliantly, but then, each member of the Homework Dog team managed to hold his or her own. The Dogs won.

"Everyone did great!" Danny said, once the team had left the stage. As captain, he felt he should encourage everyone. "Eric, you did fine. How are you feeling now?"

"Once they started asking the questions, I was really OK," he said.

"Wasn't it exciting?" Francy asked. "It was just like this thrilling race or something, like we were going down a river on a raft, and there were rapids and waterfalls, and we had to get through! Prove ourselves! Wow!!! *WHAT A RUSH!!!*" Francy gave a little hop.

Danny looked at her thoughtfully. "I think I know what you mean," he said. "It felt sort of like that for me too. It felt good."

The Homework Dogs continued to do well. In fact, they won every match they were in that day. But, so did Westside. Which brought the two teams face-to-face at the end of the day for the final and decisive match of the Great Think-Off Contest. Whichever team won the final match would be that year's champion team.

Danny gave his team a final pep talk in the wings. "All our studying really paid off," he said. "Everyone did great. Now . . ." Danny paused, searching for exactly the right words. "Ooey ka . . . Forget about that! Let's go out there and slaughter 'em!" he said.

"*YEAH!!!*" the Dogs cheered.

Ms. McCardle, who was taking a break from judging and stretching her legs in the wings, watched them from a corner. "They've done so well," she whispered to Homework, who was hovering near her head.

"Woof!" Homework agreed.

Ms. McCardle walked over to the team, with Homework invisibly at her side.

"You've done so well!" Ms. McCardle told the Dogs. "I'm very proud of you. You studied hard and you learned to work together. Remember, now," she went on, "it's not whether you win or lose, it's—"

"How you play the game!" they all said together.

"Slaughter 'em!" Tommy muttered under his breath.

"Good luck, good luck," Ms. McCardle said, and shook each team member's hand. She got to Danny last. "You're a good captain," she said. "I think . . ."

No one ever found out what Ms. McCardle thought, because at that moment, Homework found he could contain himself no longer. All day long, he had done a good job of holding his competitive nature in check—he had not given Danny a single answer. But the strain of holding back along with the frustration of sitting there watching Danny without being able to say hello, or how are you, or anything at all, finally became more than he could bear. He couldn't stand it anymore. Suddenly Danny's face was very soggy.

"What was *THAT!?!*" Danny asked, wiping slobber off his face.

"*HOME* . . ." Ms. McCardle started to say sharply to the dog, but cut herself off when she saw Danny staring at her, his mouth open wide. Afraid she'd given herself away, Ms. McCardle nervously tried to cover. "Home . . . uh, um . . . uh, home is where the heart is, that's what I always say."

The rest of the Dogs stared at her too. It seemed

like a strange thing to say at a Think-Off Contest.

"So have a good match and . . . and . . . and go home!" Ms. McCardle added quickly, then hurried to her seat.

"What an unusual person," Martha commented as the Dogs took their seats.

"Maybe even more unusual than we know," Danny said. His mind reeled. "Home . . ." Ms. Mc-Cardle had said, then she had stopped herself. Was it possible . . . ? Could it be . . . ? He knew very well that the slobber on his face didn't get there all by itself. And he knew very well what invisible dog must have put it there. Homework had always said a friend sent him. Was Ms. McCardle his friend? She always sent home notes that got him grounded. What kind of friend was that? Mrs. Curtizon was speaking into the microphone again. The match was starting. He would have to think about it later.

"Ladies and gentlemen," Mrs. Curtizon said into the mike, "we're ready to begin the final match of the Great Think-Off Contest. Let's have a big round of applause for our two finalist teams—the Westside Annihilators, and the Lewis and Clark Homework Dogs!!!"

The two opposing teams walked out onto the stage and took their seats at their respective tables. The TV cameras zoomed in and the crowd went wild, whistling, cheering, stamping their feet. Mrs. Curtizon asked the teams to stand and take a bow. The Dogs stood with their heads held high.

The match began. It was close all the way through. The Dogs got an answer, then the Westside Annihilators, then the Dogs, then the Annihilators.

"Name the civilization in South America that at one time covered the entire west coast of South America, from Ecuador to Chile," said Mrs. Curtizon.

Martha got it. "The Incas."

"Correct this sentence," said Mrs. Curtizon. "Peter and me are going to the store."

Westside got it. "Peter and *I* are going to the store."

Finally, there was time for just one more question. The score was tied. Whichever team got this question would win the whole shebang.

"What was the starting point of the Oregon Trail?" Mrs. Curtizon asked from the podium.

Danny's hand shot up. How could he not know this?

Homework, watching from his hover position next to Ms. McCardle at the judges' table, was about ready to burst his fur.

Danny was fast, but the Westside captain's hand was up a split second sooner. It was very close, but all the judges agreed that the Westside hand was up first.

"Independence, Missouri," the Westside captain answered.

Ms. McCardle nodded.

"Correct," said Mrs. Curtizon, and the Westside Annihilators won the contest.

Danny looked like someone had punched him. If only he'd been faster, his team would have won.

Homework took one look at Danny and forgot Ms. McCardle's rule about not letting anyone hear him who wasn't supposed to. He sat down and howled out loud in agony, so that everyone in the auditorium, and anyone watching at home on TV, could hear him.

Danny turned in the direction of the howl just in time to see Ms. McCardle bend over, reach down, pick up an invisible package, and run out of the auditorium.

Danny raced out after her, out the stage door of the auditorium, but he couldn't find her anywhere. There was no sign of Homework either.

CHAPTER

16

A Sunny Day

Danny would have chased Ms. McCardle, but he had no idea where to begin looking for her. He would have run to her house, but he had no idea where she lived. She never gave out her address. Some kids had wanted to make some phony phone calls to her once, but they couldn't because her telephone number was unlisted. Danny had no choice but to go back into the auditorium.

"Danny!" Eric called, waving him over to the team.

"I'm sorry, it was all my fault," Danny said, joining them.

"What?" Eric asked.

"My fault we lost," Danny explained. "I knew the answer to that last question, I really knew it, I just didn't get my hand up fast enough. I'm really sorry. Now we'll never get our revenge."

"Danny, I know you're the captain and all," Francy said, "but you know, you weren't up there alone. We were *all* up there."

"It was the job of everyone up there to answer the questions," Tommy said.

"And we didn't lose," said Martha. "We came in second."

Mrs. Curtizon was talking into the microphone again. "Will the Lewis and Clark and the Westside teams please come back onstage for the awards ceremony?" she said.

The teams came out, one last time. The Westside captain got a blue ribbon with a gold medal on it to take back to his school, and Danny got a red ribbon with a silver medal on it for Lewis and Clark. The audience cheered.

"Second," Danny whispered to Eric.

"Second isn't bad, Danny," Eric whispered back.

"It was my fault," Danny said to his family at dinner that night. "We lost, and it was my fault."

"What are you talking about?" Mom asked.

"Danny, you did great," Dad said.

"But we lost," said Danny.

"You came in second," said Grandma. "That's not losing, that's very, very good."

"We're so proud of you," said Mom.

"Want some cake?" asked Grandma.

"Woof," said Evie.

"What?" Danny asked.

"Woof," Evie repeated. "I'm a dog. A homework dog." Then, "Woof!" she said again, in a high, squeaky voice, and held up a little plastic beagle. The head reminded Danny of Homework.

"What's that?" Danny asked. "Where's Judy?"

"Judy's in the wastebasket," Evie said. "This is my new homework dog, Rex. Rex doesn't like Judy. I don't like her now either."

"*WHAT!?!*" the entire family asked together.

"I don't like her anymore," Evie said. "The hair was starting to get to me, you know what I mean?"

"Thank goodness!" said Grandma. Everyone looked at her in surprise. "I really hated that doll," Grandma said, and everyone cracked up.

"Woof!" said Evie.

"Woof!" said Danny.

"Woof!" said Rex.

Then Mom brought out a chocolate cake with the words "Congratulations to our Top Dog" written on it.

Mom handed Danny the cake knife. Everyone stood around the table, looking at Danny, waiting for him to cut the cake. It reminded Danny of the time many weeks ago when everyone had sat around the table and Danny had read them "Spring," the paper Homework had written for Danny that had gotten him an *A*.

It was basically the same scene, except something was different. When Danny had read his paper, he'd felt creepy. Now, he felt good.

"Thanks for all your help," Danny said, and cut the cake.

By the time he'd finished his third piece, he had stopped insisting he lost the match. •

"Second isn't bad," he said, licking the frosting off his fingers. "Not bad at all."

That night, when he went up to bed, Danny took a box of oatmeal cookies with him, just in case Homework dropped by. After all, this was the time Homework had always come to visit during the weeks before the Think-Off Contest.

Danny stayed up for awhile, then he fell asleep.

Homework never came.

"WOOF WOOF ARF ARF ERF!" Homework raged in Ms. McCardle's living room that night.

"I'm sorry, Homework," said Ms. McCardle. "I see how upsetting it is to you, but you absolutely cannot go see Danny now."

"ARF WOOF!"

"Why? I've been explaining it to you all night. You can't go see Danny because he needs to go through this next phase on his own. You were wonderful with him, but now he needs to find strength within himself. No one, no dog, can do that for him."

"Errrrr arrrrrr errrrr," Homework whined.

"I know you didn't get to say good-bye, and I'm sorry about that. Perhaps you could have after the contest if you hadn't let out that extraordinary howl and created such an extremely awkward situation for me."

Homework hung his head.

"Have faith that he can get through this on his own," said Ms. McCardle. "That's the best way to help Danny now. Then we'll worry about good-byes."

Monday morning, Danny rushed to school. He'd been waiting for this all weekend—a chance to talk to Ms. McCardle about Homework.

All the kids he passed on his way had nice things to say to him.

"Danny, my man! Way to go!" said one kid, as Danny hurried by.

"Hey! Great contest!" said another.

"Gave 'em a run for their money!" said yet another.

In the school yard, he saw his class hanging out together.

"O Captain! My Captain!" Tommy sang out when he saw him, and everybody cheered.

Danny looked around. Practically everyone in the school was wearing a T-shirt with a dog painted on the front. The kids who wanted to look really cool had their hands up to their eyes like blinders and were walking around with their heads bent down. Each team member was surrounded by his or her own circle of fans.

"We did the best we could," Danny said, then he rushed into the school. He ran into his classroom. Ms. McCardle was seated at her desk.

Ms. McCardle looked up as he came in. "Oh, Danny," she said. "I'm glad you're here. I have some news that might interest you about graduation."

"Ms. McCardle, you know I can't . . . can't graduate," Danny sputtered. "You *know* that. Except for a couple of weeks at the end of March, I haven't turned in any homework since February. But I'm getting sidetracked. There's something I really have to ask you. Or tell you. I know you sent me a . . ."

Ms. McCardle cut him off. "You're quite right, Danny, I shouldn't pass you. But you earned so much extra credit for all the work you did getting ready for the contest, that you will be able to pass with the rest of your class, if you want to."

"What do you *mean*, you're going to let me *pass*?"

Danny asked. He was outraged. "It's not *fair!* I mean, I studied for the contest, but that was *extra-curricular! I didn't do any homework! I shouldn't be able to pass!*"

"Oh, but all of the team members got extra credit for being on the team, didn't you know that?" Ms. McCardle asked.

"No! Of course I didn't know that! I never would have been on the team if I'd known that!" Danny exclaimed.

"Oh, well, I guess you were in the bathroom or something when I announced it," Ms. McCardle said. "You see, even though you haven't done any work since February, the extra work you did with your team brings your overall grade up to a *D*, but still, in your case, I'm going to let you . . ."

"*You tricked me!*" Danny stormed. "First you tried to trick me with a dog, but it didn't work. OK, it was cool having a talking dog help me with things, and when I *wanted* to study, it was great, but now—this—this is too much. I think it's a dirty trick."

"What dog, Danny?" asked Ms. McCardle, smiling. Her eyes blinked fast behind the frames of her oversized glasses. "What are you talking about?"

"Of course you'll never admit it, I should have expected that," Danny answered. "But I know."

Ms. McCardle looked at Danny. "You keep interrupting me," she said. "You won't let me finish a sentence. You see, I'm not tricking you. I was about to say I would let you decide. About whether or not to get promoted to sixth grade, I mean."

Danny shook his head quickly, as if he hadn't heard right.

"You see, Danny, I really want this to be your decision. My goodness, you must have studied every second of your life after you joined the team in order to do so well in the contest. You did a good job, and you were a good captain. Don't you feel the littlest bit proud?"

"We didn't get our revenge," Danny said, "but, yeah, it feels pretty good."

"I always say there's no feeling in the world like the feeling you get when you know you worked hard and did a good job," Ms. McCardle said. "Doesn't it make you feel that you could conquer bigger things?"

Danny said nothing.

Ms. McCardle stood for a moment, looking at him. "Growing up is just part of life," she finally said. "Whether you graduate or not, you'll still grow up eventually."

"I think that's what my mom said once," Danny said.

Ms. McCardle nodded. "If you want to graduate," she said, "come to the ceremony. If not, I'll see you again next year."

The bell rang. Ms. McCardle sat down at her desk and took out some papers. Kids started rushing through the doors. Danny took his seat.

Homework hovered invisibly next to Ms. McCardle's right ear and whimpered softly.

The last two weeks of school, Danny's class did a lot of cool things. Danny didn't do any of them.

In science, they all made rockets and launched them in the playground. Danny watched, sure that his rocket would have flown great, if he'd made one, but he hadn't.

"Come on! Make a rocket!" the kids said.

Danny just stood there.

For social studies, the kids put on a pageant about their favorite Native American cultures, with costumes. Danny watched. As a person with experience as a captain, he knew he would have done a good job playing a great Native American chief, but he stayed in the audience.

"At least be a buffalo," Tommy had said.

"I can't," Danny had answered.

"Gimme a break," Tommy had said as he walked away.

After a while, the kids stopped encouraging Danny to join in the different activities. Everyone left him alone.

Danny watched everything from a distance. Once in a while he looked around, hoping for, but never getting a glimpse of Homework. Otherwise, Danny did nothing.

"Hagh, hagh, hagh!" Mr. Jessup coughed into the microphone on graduation day. Perhaps he coughed a little more loudly than usual, due to the excitement of sending yet another group of fifth graders forth from the safe, homey hallways of Lewis and Clark to the great wide world of middle school.

The friends and families of the graduates filled the auditorium, the fifth-grade teachers sat in chairs placed at the front of the stage, and the graduates themselves waited expectantly in the hallway. Everyone was chatting quietly, waiting for the graduation ceremony to begin.

"Hagh, hagh, ha . . ."

Ms. McCardle grabbed the microphone from Mr. Jessup and cut him off.

"Mr. Jessup would like your attention, please," Ms. McCardle said brusquely into the microphone.

"Ladies, gentlemen, and children," Mr. Jessup said, grabbing back the mike. Every kid over the age of six groaned. "It gives me great pleasure to present to you this year's graduating class!"

The audience applauded, and the school music teacher, Mr. Gruber, struck up some processional music at the piano. This year, instead of "Pomp and Circumstance," the traditional music for graduations, the fifth graders had talked Mr. Gruber into playing "How Much Is that Doggy in the Window?" in honor of the Homework Dogs. The music teacher, who had really grown to hate "Pomp and Circumstance" over the years, thought it was a brilliant idea.

"Da-DAH-DAH-DAH, DAAAAAH da-da-da da-duh . . ." went the piano, and Mr. Jessup went berserk. He walked quickly over to Mr. Gruber at the piano and whispered in his ear.

Mr. Gruber stopped playing and turned to Mr. Jessup indignantly. "I composed this *myself*," he said, loud enough for everyone in the auditorium to hear, "es*pecially* for this year's graduation!"

"Oh, I beg your pardon," Mr. Jessup said, flustered. "But it sounds a bit like 'How Much Is that Doggy in the Window?' don't you think?"

"It's *supposed* to sound like that," Mr. Gruber said icily, and resumed playing "How Much Is that Doggy in the Window?" as solemnly as possible. Then he played variations of "Git Along Little Doggy," just to break things up.

The members of the audience were having a hard time controlling their laughter. The graduates standing close enough to the doors of the auditorium to hear what was going on were hysterical. Mr. Jessup went back to the podium and started calling the graduates' names from an alphabetical list, and alphabetically, the graduates entered, laughing, waving to their families, and generally having a wonderful time.

The mood was contagious. Kids who hadn't heard the interchange between Mr. Jessup and Mr. Gruber started laughing, too, just for the fun of it. The audience started clapping in time to Mr. Gruber's music, and as the graduates' names were called, they boogied down the center aisle of the auditorium to get their diplomas, shake hands with their teachers and Mr. Jessup, and take their seats on stage.

Danny's name was way down on the list, since his last name was Wilder. Mom, Dad, Grandma, Evie, and Rex were in the audience, waiting to see Danny march down the aisle.

"Susan Charney," Mr. Jessup called, and Susan took her diploma. There were ninety-eight more names on the list.

Three blocks away, a wadded-up paper basketball sailed across Danny's bedroom.

Throw, whoosh. Basket.

Throw, whoosh. Basket.

Throw, whoosh. Basket.

Danny sighed, and shifted his position on the bed.

"Lance Gueraldo," read Mr. Jessup from the podium.

Throw, whoosh. Basket.

Danny shot one basket after another and thought about the last two weeks of school. His class had done such cool things. Why hadn't he done any of them? It didn't make any sense. Ms. McCardle had left the choice up to him—whether to graduate or not—so it wouldn't have mattered one way or the other if he'd participated or not.

He could have done all of it, but not now. Now it was over. Now it was too late.

"Joan Mentoff," read Mr. Jessup.

Danny crumpled up a sheet of paper but he didn't throw it. He sat very still. The house was quiet. The whole family was at the graduation, waiting to see him walk down the aisle. They didn't know he'd only pretended to go to school early and that he'd snuck back to the house as soon as they were gone.

Danny scrunched the piece of crumpled paper tighter in his hand. He looked out the window. The sun was shining. A light breeze was blowing through the trees in the front yard. The leaves bounced and fluttered.

Danny sat up.

"It's a nice, sunny day!" he said out loud, "And I'm sitting in here, all by myself, throwing paper through a hanger!"

"Heidi Reynolds," read Mr. Jessup.

"THIS IS BORING!!!" Danny yelled. "I HATE THIS!!!"

He tore the crumpled-up paper he'd been holding into tiny bits and tossed them in the trash. Basket!

"*WARP-FREE?*" Danny shouted. "*WARP-FREE? WARP-FREE is the worst warp of all!*"

"Danny Wilder," Mr. Jessup read from the podium. Danny did not appear. Mr. Jessup looked up.

"Danny Wilder," he repeated, a little louder. Still no Danny. "Is Danny sick today, or some—"

"HERE I AM!!!" Danny shouted, racing down the aisle. "HERE I COME!!!"

Danny took his diploma from Mr. Jessup and waved it over his head. Then he went down the line of teachers standing next to Mr. Jessup, shaking hands as he went. When he got to Ms. McCardle, she grasped his hand tightly in hers. She smiled. Danny smiled back.

"Thanks," said Danny. "Thanks for everything."

"I should thank you," said Ms. McCardle. "You taught me a lot."

"Will I see him again?" Danny asked.

Ms. McCardle didn't answer.

The auditorium was silent. Everyone had heard the interchange between Danny and Ms. McCardle, but no one knew what it meant.

"Congratulations!" Ms. McCardle exclaimed, and the audience applauded politely.

There was only one fifth grader left, a Z kid, Adam Zibursky, and he had been standing on the stage next to Mr. Jessup during the conversation between Danny and Ms. McCardle. He didn't even wait for Mr. Jessup to call his name, he just grabbed his diploma, shook everyone's hand and sat down. The audience applauded again, and the speeches began.

Danny heard them only as a background for his own thoughts. What would it be like? he thought. The middle school was big. Would he get lost? Would the teachers be nice? The school had a basketball team. Maybe he should try out. Maybe he just would.

Then it was over.

The kids started cheering and whistling, jumping up and down, shaking each other's hands, telling each other it truly *was* the best class ever. Eric launched into a heated discussion of the current presidential administration with Ms. McCardle; Francy and Martha tried to decide which foreign language they would take in middle school; Tommy tried to walk up the rear wall of the stage; Mr. Gruber, the piano teacher, launched into the theme song from the movie "Dog Day Afternoon"; Mom, Dad, Grandma, Evie, and Rex swayed back and forth together in the audience, dancing in their seats; Mr. Jessup continually cleared his throat into the microphone; and Danny tossed his diploma in the air and caught it, over and over again.

On about the fifty-fifth or fifty-sixth throw, something happened. The diploma stopped, suspended in midair for a moment, then floated gently down until it was right in front of Danny's face.

"Hi, Homework," Danny said, taking the diploma from the invisible dog's mouth.

"I've come to say good-bye," said Homework, making himself visible to Danny as he hovered next to him.

"*Good-bye?*" Danny asked. "What do you mean— *good-bye?*"

"I mean, good-bye," said Homework. "You don't need me anymore. There are other kids who do."

"But I do need you," Danny said. "Or I might. What if I need help in middle school? What if I decide to flunk again? You know, high school's only a few years away."

Homework gently nuzzled Danny's chin and said, "You'll be fine."

Danny hugged the hovering dog. "I missed you," Danny whispered. "I thought I might not see you again."

"I missed you, too," said Homework. "You know, you were a real pain for awhile, but you're basically a good kid." Homework gave Danny's left ear one last, quick slobber and whispered, "Good-bye. You really will be just fine."

Then he was gone.

"Home . . ." Danny started to call, but didn't bother to finish. Homework was gone. Danny knew he would not be back.

Danny dropped his arms, which he was still holding out as if he were hugging Homework. He looked around at the commotion in the auditorium, and he realized that in a few minutes he, too, would be gone. He wouldn't disappear the way Homework had, but he would walk through the doors of the school—the school where he had come every school day of his life since he was five years old—and he would not be back. Oh, maybe he'd come back once in a while, to see Evie in some ridiculous kindergarten play or something, or to visit Ms. McCardle, but he wouldn't be back as a student, he wouldn't ever really be part of the place again.

And Danny also knew, as he watched Tommy Lewis almost do a complete somersault off the wall, that Homework was right.

Danny knew he would be just fine.